EVAN'S WISH

THE BULLSEYE CLUB BOOK 1

ROBIN STONE

EVAN'S WISH

Can he separate business from pleasure?

Hardworking Evan is proud of his maintenance job in the new apartment building in town. He's saving up to buy a house, so his brother Matt has a place to live when he graduates from college. Matt's trying to stay sober, and Evan wants to help him get a solid footing with a safe place to live.

Savvy real estate agent Brooke asks Evan to escort her to an event. She's attracted to Evan, and after a pleasant date, she wants to see him again. Evan is not like the usual lawyers and businessmen she dates, and their attraction is undeniable.

But When Brooke offers to pay Evan to escort her to more events, he hesitates. He feels out of place at formal events, but he's getting attached to the curvy brunette, and he needs the money. Can Evan learn to separate business from pleasure?

REVIEWS

Praise for Robin Stone's writing

"...My emotions ran the gamut from heartbreaking fear to utter joy...Tumultuous at times, but always sensual. The conclusion was the only viable ending, and it was a stunner!" - Lori, wee bit o' whiskey on *Landscaper in Paradise*

"The continuous emotional turmoil is so real to life that it will leave you in tears one minute and laughing the next. A beautiful story with a beautiful ending..." - Queenie, Amazon, on *Landscaper in Paradise*

"In addition to sex so hot it made me squirm in my chair, I was impressed with Stone's clean, slick writing..." - Patient Lee, Writerotica, on *The Landscaper Series*

"...scorching and seductive reading. Naughty, fun and deliciously erotic. This will take you no time at all to digest, just make sure you can do so in private, ideally with some ice on hand!" - Ruthie Taylor, Wicked Reads Reviews

"...These would be great stories to read at night with a significant other beside you to share in the love, the heartache, the passion and the deep emotions of the characters involved." - Shadow Knight, Amazon, on *The Blue Collar Collection*

"Trying to get dinner going and can't stop reading this. Just a sampler, but I want to read more. Dinner is probably sandwiches now." - m torres, Amazon, on *The Landscaper*

ONE

I climbed my aluminum ladder for the hundredth time that day, but my mind was on the sexy brunette pacing the kitchen floor.

Concentrate. Just install this alarm, and you can go to lunch.

I was going around to the condos in the building and adding a new alarm speaker to the interior of each unit. The high-end building was less than a year old, and the hallways still smelled of fresh paint. The fire alarm in the hallways had gone off a few times, but some of the residents said they couldn't hear it inside the units, so we had to install speakers inside each condo.

The electricians had already been in to run the wires. I just had to hang up a decorative faceplate and help test the alarms. Tightening one of the screws, I dropped the second one on the floor. I cursed under my breath and climbed down the ladder, scanning the floor for the tiny screw.

The woman talked on her phone while she paced. The scent of her floral perfume filled my nostrils. She looked all business in her silky white blouse, fitted beige skirt, and heels.

"I know," she said into her phone. "Yes."

She crouched down and picked up the screw. I got a nice view of her shapely calves, but tried not to stare. When she held up the screw, I held out my hand, and she dropped the screw into my palm.

"Thanks," I whispered.

She gave me a quick nod. I climbed back up the ladder and installed the screw.

The view I had from the ladder was distracting. The woman had bent over to shake some food into a pet bowl, and her shaking movements made her curvy ass sway. My screwdriver stopped midair while I watched.

She cradled her phone against her ear and picked up the pet's water bowl to refill at the sink. I heard a loud male voice on the phone. I looked back at the grate so she wouldn't notice me staring.

The truth was, I'd noticed 3B—Brooke Sinclair—on my first day of work three months ago. She was walking briskly through the lobby, her phone glued to her ear. She nodded at me as I mopped the lobby floor. I held the door open once when she was carrying in bags of groceries, and she gave me a brilliant smile, causing my skin to heat beneath my uniform.

I think she did something with real estate because I heard her saying things like "lakefront property" and "quartz counter-tops." She was always dressed in skirts or fitted pantsuits and wore pearls or gold necklaces. She had to have money to live in a place like this.

"We'll talk about it in the meeting tomorrow," she said.

She sounded annoyed, her heels clicking on the tile floor as she paced. She had curves I liked, and her clothing accentuated every one. I liked a woman with meat on her bones.

I pictured filling my hands with her nice, round butt, hauling her up against me and sliding my hands up her ribcage.

I looked back at my work, knowing I shouldn't be thinking this way about one of the residents. But I hadn't dated in a while, and this woman was filling my thoughts every time I saw her.

"Right. Yes, that closing is next week."

A gray cat sauntered into the kitchen, purring and rubbing itself against her legs. She bent down and gave the cat a scratch behind the ears.

"Hey, punkin," she whispered. "You're a good girl."

The cat went to her bowl and started eating.

"Listen," she said in a take-charge voice I liked. "I need to let you go. I'll see you in the office later. Yes. Goodbye." She hung up and placed her phone on the counter. "Sorry about that."

"No problem, Miss Sinclair."

She gave me her wide smile, and her pretty face lit up.

"Please, call me Brooke."

"No problem, Miss...uh, Brooke," I said. "I'm almost finished."

I concentrated on screwing the new speaker faceplate on, mindful she was still watching me. I willed my skin to stay cool as I worked the screwdriver, awareness zinging through my body.

The units in this building sold for over four-hundred-fifty-thousand dollars. I was saving for a house of my own, but couldn't imagine being able to afford that much—not that I even liked the building. The soaring, glass-filled lobby always seemed cold and impersonal. The individual units were okay, depending on how the owners decorated.

Units owned by single men could be pretty bland, but I liked Brooke's unit. She had family photos on the walls, colored throw pillows and area rugs, bright blue and yellow bowls. Lots of books, and even a few board games. It felt happy and relaxed.

I put my screwdriver into my belt, climbed down, and folded the ladder shut.

"All done," I said. "They'll send out a notice before they test the alarms."

"Thank you, Evan," she said.

I looked up, surprised that she knew my name. She pointed to my embroidered name tag.

"Oh, right," I said.

Most people didn't even bother to learn our names. I hoisted the ladder up and opened her door. I put the ladder in the hall and turned to grab my toolbox.

"Do you like working here, Evan?" she asked.

"Sure." I picked up my toolbox. "Nice new building. Nice people."

She stepped closer, and I got a better look at her face—pretty blue eyes, long eyelashes, and a few freckles on her nose and cheeks. I thought she might be older than me, but not by much. It was hard to tell with some people. She wore a gold chain around her neck, and small gold earrings.

"Where did you work before you came here?" she asked.

"At the apartment complexes on Second Street."

"I know them. A builder is looking to put up a new apartment building at the vacant lot at the end of that street."

"Oh yeah?" I asked. "You know the builder?"

"I'm a real estate agent." She walked to a kitchen drawer, took out a business card, and handed it to me. "I work for Turner Real Estate."

I shifted my toolbox to my left hand and reached out with my right. Her fingertips brushed mine, and she drew in a sharp breath at our touch. My pulse pounded, and I looked down at the card to break our intense eye contact.

"Thanks." I tucked the card into my tool belt. "I'm looking to buy in a year or so."

"Good! Why don't you give me your number?"

"Sure."

She pushed a pad of paper and a pen toward me on the counter, and I wrote down my info.

Silence stretched between us. Her gaze dropped to my chest, then slid back up to my mouth. It had been a while, but I knew when I was being checked out.

And I liked it.

Her blue eyes met mine again, and her full lips quirked.

"It's been a pleasure, Evan." She closed the door behind me.

I picked up my ladder and whistled as I walked down the hall to the next unit, thinking about blue eyes and curves, hoping I'd see her again soon.

TWO

Thursday night and Cooper's Tavern was buzzing with activity. A Red Sox game played on the flat screen above the bar, loud male voices talked over the sports announcers, and patrons walked by on the creaky wooden floor. Neon beer signs glowed with the names of beers that weren't made anymore.

The bar had dark paneled walls, uneven tables, and worn-down bar stools from the work boots of carpenters, painters, and guys like me and my roommate, Liam. Once in a while, a few hipsters wandered in, looking for craft beers and organic pizza, but they usually left disappointed and didn't come back.

That was just how we liked it here.

Tom, the crusty owner and main bartender, kept the place clean enough. It was dark and dated, but it was like a second home to me, Liam, and the guys in the Bullseye Club.

"Quiet, you assholes!" Liam yelled. "I can't hear the game!"

After work, I'd picked up Liam in my truck, and we headed straight here to watch the game and get some chow. Liam still worked in maintenance at the run-down apartment buildings where we met five years ago.

My stomach cramped with guilt every time I picked him up

at the rear entrance next to the rusty dumpster. Liam had a car, but was saving up for new tires. I offered to loan him the money with my extra pay, but he turned me down.

"No way," he said. "That's money for your house. I'm not takin' it. Quit feelin' guilty. There was only one job open, and you got it. I'll get my chance one of these days."

I told Liam I'd recommend him if another job opened up, but so far, it hadn't. I tried to make up for the difference in pay, buying Liam's pizza or paying for his beers once in a while. But I made sure to put my extra pay into a savings account for a house. The account was growing painfully slow until I got this new job.

A few minutes later, our buddies Max and Drew joined us, and we put in orders for burgers, beer, and fries. Max had a stocky build and scarred hands from welding. Drew was lanky and always wore the same lucky Sox cap during the season. He was a drywall installer.

I half-listened to their conversation, keeping my eyes on the score. The Sox were down by three, and the guys were getting loud.

"You're a dipshit," Max said. "You couldn't *pay* me to get married."

"I'm not getting married. I haven't even asked her!" Drew said.

Max was an avowed bachelor, and Drew's girlfriend was dropping major hints about rings.

"Just wait," Max said. "First, she starts talking about rings, then she'll start talking about dresses and renting the Carlisle for the reception."

Drew groaned. "I can't afford that hotel! I was hoping we could get married in her parent's backyard or somethin'."

"No girl wants to get married in some back yard," Max said.

Jessa, the tavern's long-suffering waitress, came over with our tray of burgers and fries.

"And I suppose you know exactly what women want, right Max?" she asked, nudging his arm.

Drew and Liam and the guys sitting at the bar laughed.

"You know it, baby," Max said, wiggling his dark brows.

Jessa had a boyfriend and was off-limits, but that never stopped guys from trying. She tossed her head, her blonde ponytail flinging over her shoulder.

"Leave her alone, Max!"

Tom, the grey-haired, gruff bartender scowled as he polished the bar.

I picked up a fry and tossed it at Max. "Yeah, asshole."

Max turned to me. "What the hell do you know about it? You don't even have a girlfriend."

Liam elbowed me in the ribs. "Yeah, been a while."

"Shut up," I muttered. "I met someone today."

There was a beat of silence, and several heads swiveled in my direction.

"Atta boy!"

"'Bout goddamn time!"

"Who is she?"

I wiped my mouth with a napkin, stalling for time. Heat crept up my neck.

"Her name is Brooke, and trust me, you animals don't know her."

"Brooke, huh?" Liam asked. "Where did you meet her?"

The guys at the bar cheered at the TV. Liam glanced at the screen for a few seconds, but I wasn't off the hook.

"You haven't mentioned a girl named Brooke," Liam said, frowning. "Thought you told me everything."

"I do," I said. "It's just... I met her at work, and I think she might be interested."

"At work?" Liam asked. "She on staff there?"

"No." I dipped a fry in ketchup. "She lives in the building."

"Uh oh!" Max's dark brows knitted together. "She lives there? This girl is *way* outta your league."

"Why do you say that?" I asked.

"Come on, Evan. You know how much those units cost. Almost half a mil. She lives alone? No boyfriend? No roommate?"

"I'm not sure. She was talking to a guy on the phone, but it sounded like business. It didn't look like a guy lived there."

"So, she carries a mortgage for that place on her own. She dress nice? Have nice jewelry?"

I squirmed in my chair. "What's your point?"

Liam shook his head. "Women like that don't give guys like us a second look. Never works out. Worlds apart."

"That's bullshit!" I said. "She was checking me out today. And when I run into her in the hallway, well..."

"What?" Liam asked.

I thought back to Brooke and her smile when I held open the lobby door for her. She seemed friendly, as if she'd smile at anyone who opened the door.

But what about that hitch in her breath today when our fingers touched?

"She gave me her card," I said, as if that settled it.

"Oh yeah?" Max asked. "Where does she work?"

"She's a real estate agent. Turner Real Estate."

The guys laugh-snorted and rolled their eyes.

"I told her I was looking to buy a house soon." I shoved my basket of fries away. "She seemed nice. She was definitely checkin' me out."

Max whacked the back of my head. "They sell mansions at Turner Estates with heated pools, five-car garages, and tennis courts. Nothing you could afford even if you saved up for a million years."

Shit. I didn't know that.

"This girl was friendly because she wanted your business," Max said. "Or a referral."

"Hey," Liam said. "Maybe she does like him! Quit bustin' his balls!"

Good old Liam, he always had my back.

"Nah," Drew said. "She probably has a boyfriend who's a lawyer or something. She wouldn't go out with a maintenance guy in her building."

Jessa came over to pick up some empties. "What are you guys yammering about?"

"Evan likes a girl who lives in his building. She works at Turner Real Estate."

Jessa cocked her head. "That's the one where they sell the mansions, right?"

I nodded, waiting for Jessa to give me shit. She could dish it out as bad as any of the guys. She looked at me.

"Why not?" she asked. "You still have all your hair and teeth. You're a good catch, unlike these idiots."

That set off another round of raucous arguments and insults. Jessa laughed and walked away with our empties. The Sox must've scored again because a fresh round of cheers went up.

"Damn, it's loud in here tonight," Liam said.

I yanked out my wallet and tossed some bills on the table. "No kidding. I'm gonna go home."

"What, already?" Liam asked. "We just got here! Game's not over!"

I shrugged. "I should call Matt. I haven't heard from him for a few days. Call me if you need a ride later."

He waved at me. "I'm fine. Go do your thing."

I said goodbye to everyone on the way out the door. I was relieved to get out of the hot, stuffy bar and hit the cool night air outside. The street was pretty quiet. I thought about Brooke as I walked back to my truck.

Was she just being nice? Just looking for business? I knew that real estate agents could turn on the charm around people, but there was something more there, I could feel it. Maybe she had a boyfriend. Maybe it was the guy on the phone.

When I got home, I went straight to my room and turned on the radio to listen to the game. I had the smaller bedroom in the apartment, but I didn't mind. Liam lived here first, and he was happy for me to move in and share the rent and utilities. The apartment was dated, but good enough with a decent kitchen and a large living room.

I sat at my small desk and brought up my savings account on my computer. I looked at the balance, saw the amount added from this week's check, and sighed. The account was growing, but it felt like it was taking forever to save up for a decent down payment.

I turned down the radio, then picked up my phone to call Matty.

"Yo," he said, rock music blaring through the phone. "What's up?"

"Matty?" I asked. "I can barely hear you."

"Evan? That you? Sorry, let me go in the other room. The guys are over." The music faded a little. "What's up?"

"Just checking in to see how you're doing."

"I know." There was a hint of annoyance in his voice. "Listen, can we talk another time? We're going to another apartment to watch the game."

"Okay," I said. "Call me back soon."

"I will."

The phone went silent. I hung up and turned up the radio. I

took out Brooke's card. Curious, I looked up Turner Real Estate on my computer, scrolling through the agents until I found Brooke's photo. I clicked on it and saw a list of all her awards and accomplishments—top seller of the year, number one agent in the tri-county area, top sales for the month.

Brooke was a go-getter. I liked that, but the guys were right, the houses on this site were expensive as hell. I scrolled past a two-million-dollar home on a lake with a dock, and a log home listed at just under a million. The least expensive house I found was half a million.

Closing the site, I opened another that listed more modest homes. I scrolled to see if there was anything new since the last time I looked, comparing prices and square footage.

Liam must be having fun with the guys since he didn't come back early. I watched the rest of the game in the living room, then got ready for bed. I'd climbed into bed and was starting to get sleepy when Liam came home. He gave my door a quick tap on the way to his room, his way of saying goodnight when he came home after me.

I adjusted my pillow and pulled up my covers, thinking about Brooke and her curves, imagining the warmth of her body against mine. Her skin and hair would smell incredible up close. I had to find out more about her. Screw it, I was gonna ask her out tomorrow. The worst she could do was say no.

But somehow, I knew she wouldn't.

THREE

The next morning, I didn't see Brooke at all as I went about my morning duties. I mopped the lobby floor, then cleaned the glass on the entry doors, looking up each time I heard a woman's heels click through the lobby.

She was probably at work or off showing houses. I couldn't expect her to be home just because I wanted to talk to her, and it seemed creepy to knock on her door and ask her out.

I tried to put her out of my mind. An hour later, two guys from the fire department came to help test the new speakers. I nodded when I saw Travis. I knew him from the bar.

"Hey, Trav," I said. "How's it hangin?"

He chuckled. "Heard you were sweet on someone named Brooke."

My neck warmed. "What the hell? How could you know about that?"

Travis was a tall, blonde, strapping guy who made the ladies' pants fall down with a flash of his smile. His deep laugh boomed through the cavernous lobby.

"I went to Cooper's last night," he said. "The Three Musketeers told me all about it."

Drew, Max, and Liam—those assholes.

"I see it's true since your ears are red." He thumped me on the back. "Ask her out! Who the hell cares what she does for work?"

I rolled my eyes. "Easy for you to say."

It was true—I'd seen the way women acted around firefighters. They didn't act like that around maintenance guys.

A text had gone out yesterday, telling the residents the hall alarms would be going off during the day. A few people opened their doors and looked into the hallway when the alarms went off, but most people were at work. Brooke's door stayed shut during the test, but I was glad. I wanted to talk to her in private.

I was in the break room, eating a late lunch around one. The alarm testing took a while, and the other guys had already eaten when I heard a knock on the open door. I looked up mid-bite and nearly choked when I saw Brooke standing there.

I swallowed and stood, brushing my hands on my pants. She looked gorgeous and expensive in a light blue pantsuit, a strand of pearls, her hair tied up off her neck. She looked out of place in the industrial grey and dull white of the break room.

"Hi," I said.

"Hi. One of the other guys—Frank—said you were in here."

"Yeah, it's fine. I was just eating a late lunch." I walked over to her.

She reached up and fiddled with her pearls. "Evan, I was wondering if you'd like to go to an event with me tonight."

I blinked. Did I hear her right? One of her dark brows was raised, and a smile quirked her lips.

"What kind of event?"

"I'm going to a cocktail party at seven with some colleagues."

I shifted in my work boots. "A cocktail party. Okay."

My shirt suddenly felt scratchy. The clock ticked loudly on the wall.

"I'm sorry for putting you on the spot," she said. "I just thought we had a moment yesterday." She looked me squarely in the eyes and stepped closer.

I caught a whiff of her flowery perfume, and my pulse sped up. Damn, her lips were sexy, nice and plump, with just a hint of pale lipstick. She had a freckle on her neck.

"I don't want to step on anyone's toes," I said, thinking about the male voice on the phone.

"Oh, you're not." Her gaze dropped to my mouth. "I'm not seeing anyone. Are you?"

"No, I'm not seeing anyone."

She lifted her right hand and traced my name tag with her fingertip.

"I'm glad to hear that, Evan."

Her lashes were so long, and I could see her pulse beating in her neck, and for one fleeting moment, I pictured myself kissing that freckle, breathing in her skin and perfume. I licked my lips and leaned in a little, but my radio squawked, and we both jumped.

"Evan?" Frank asked, his voice tinny. "You finished with lunch? I need you on four."

The spell broken, she took a step back. I grabbed my radio from my belt, lifted it to my mouth, and pressed the button.

"Yeah, Frank. I'll be up in five." I put the radio back on my belt. "Sorry about that."

"It's fine."

I stuck my thumb into my belt loop. "Should I pick you up?"

She reached into her jacket pocket and took out a card.

"Here's the address. Meet me there at seven?"

I took the card from her, and our fingertips brushed.

There it was again, the little zap, the same connection between us from yesterday, but today it was more intense.

I glanced at the address. It was the fancy hotel in town where Drew's girlfriend wanted to get married—The Carlisle. I flipped over the card and saw her business info.

"Sure," I said. "See you at seven."

"Looking forward to it." She smiled and walked back into the hallway.

I listened as the click of her heels faded as she walked away. I took a chance and stuck my head out of the doorway, watching her hips sway as she walked away.

Brooke had a sexy but confident walk. Her dark hair was tied up in a white comb on the back of her head. How would it feel to pull that comb out and watch her hair tumble down her shoulders? What would her face look like when I leaned in to kiss her? Would she close her eyes? Or would she leave those blue eyes open and watch me lean in?

She'd watch me lean in, I decided. Those blue eyes would focus on my mouth until we were almost touching, then her lids would drift shut as I pressed my lips to hers.

I went back to the table and finished eating, thinking about Brooke and wondering how the hell I was going to fit in at some fancy cocktail party.

* * *

I GOT out of work at four and went to the bank for some cash on the way home. After an early dinner with Liam, I took a shower, and by six-fifteen I was dressed. I was standing in front of the bathroom mirror combing my hair when Liam appeared in the hallway.

"What?" I asked. "Do I look okay? I wish we had a full-length mirror."

He snorted. "What for? All we wear is jeans or uniforms."

"Well, it wouldn't kill us to dress up once in a while."

I was wearing my one good outfit from my cousin's engagement party—black pants, black shoes, a blue button-down shirt, and a blazer. My cousin had dragged me out shopping, telling me I wasn't going to her engagement party in "another damn pair of jeans." I had to admit I liked the outfit, but I didn't really have anywhere else to wear it.

I was trying unsuccessfully to get a lock of hair on the back of my head to lie down. It stuck up ever since I was a kid. I wet my hand under the faucet and tried to mash it down.

"You should let my sister cut your hair," Liam said. "She's really good with men's haircuts. All the guys in my family go to her. She'd give you the family discount, you know."

"My haircuts are fine."

I didn't trust Liam's sister with my hair. I'd seen Liam come home with some botched haircuts while she was training in beauty school.

"She's really good now," he said.

"Sure," I said. "She needs another decade of practice."

Liam crossed his arms. "So, what are you gonna do if she asks you out again? You only have that one outfit."

I shot him a look. "I know. I haven't thought that far ahead."

"Obviously."

Deciding my hair was as good as it was gonna get, I left and took my time on the ride downtown. I always liked spring in New England—green grass, flowering bushes, and birds chirping—such a relief from the dreary brown and grey scenery of winter.

Traffic was light downtown, and I found a parking spot on a side road just off Main Street. Most of the shops were closed and dimly lit, but the hotel's front windows cast yellow light onto the sidewalk. I walked up to the glass doors and looked inside. An employee was talking on the phone at the desk, but I didn't see anyone else. I reached for the door handle when I heard heels clicking on the sidewalk.

"Evan."

Brooke was wearing a stylish raincoat over her pantsuit and carrying a purse.

"Oh, hi."

She met me at the door. Her cheeks were pink, and her eyes looked bright.

"You look so handsome," she said.

I looked down, almost forgetting I was wearing nice clothes. "Thanks. You look nice, too."

"Thank you."

Opening the door, I let her walk in front of me. Leading us to the coat check area, she started to shrug out of her coat. My fingers brushed against her neck, the skin impossibly soft.

I carried it over to the coat check girl, and she gave me a tag with a number on it. I spotted a small tip jar on the counter and paused. Did I give her a tip now or when I picked up the coat later? A cold sweat broke out on my neck. I wasn't cut out for this sorta thing. I quickly fished out my wallet and stuffed a bill in her jar.

"Thank you," the girl said. "Have a nice evening."

I turned back to Brooke.

"This way," she said. "It's in the Breakwater Room."

I walked beside her on the plush patterned carpet.

"Have you ever been in this hotel?" she asked.

"A long time ago, but not since the renovations. It looks so different."

"The construction company did a fantastic job. They found some of the old doors in the basement, fixed them up, and rehung them."

"Wow."

"This party is to show the plans for the renovation of the second-floor reception room. The wall has an enormous mural that was painted in 1865. It needs extensive renovations. The hotel hired a company to..." She stopped. "Listen to me, I'm babbling."

"No, not at all," I said. "You have a passion for buildings."

"I love selling real estate."

"How long have you been doing that?"

"Eleven years."

I scanned her face again, trying to figure out how old she was. When she smiled, she had a few crinkles around her eyes, but a lot of people had those. She wore makeup—just a hint of eyeshadow and pale pink lipstick. I figured she was older than me.

We entered a large room filled with chattering people and servers carrying trays. A waitress approached us.

"Champagne?"

"Yes, thank you," Brooke said, taking a glass.

"Sure, thanks."

I'd never had champagne before, but there was always a first time. Brooke took a sip, and so did I.

"You don't like it," Brooke said.

I looked down at the glass. Somehow I thought champagne would taste better with the way people carried on about it.

"No."

"And this is the good stuff," she said. "Well, it's not for everyone."

"Guess I just prefer a cold beer."

"So do I," she said.

"Really?" I smirked. "I'd love to see that."

"It's a deal," she said. "Although you won't find any here tonight."

I glanced at the well-dressed crowd sipping champagne and

chatting. Several women wore suits like Brooke, and all the men wore suits and ties. *Why the hell didn't I think to put on a tie?*

"Brooke, darling, hello."

An older woman with grey hair approached, holding a glass of champagne. She wore a red shirt beneath her fitted black suit, and diamonds glittered on her wrists, fingers, and ears.

"Hello, Camille. How are you?" Brooke asked.

"I'm fine." She looked me up and down. "Who is this handsome fellow?"

A quick flash of fear showed on Brooke's face. "This is Evan—"

"Evan Handler," I said, offering my hand.

Camille shook my hand and grinned. "Delightful. Have you two seen the plans yet?"

"No, not yet," Brooke said. "It's a little crowded over there."

A waitress passed by, collecting glasses. I handed her mine.

"I'll see you tomorrow, Brooke," she said. "Evan, nice to meet you."

"Nice to meet you," I said.

"I work with Camille," Brooke said. "Some of the people here are coworkers, or they work in competing offices."

Brooke put her hand on my arm and tried to guide us through the crowd, but we were stopped every few feet. A tall man in a dark suit and glasses approached. I noticed his eyes scanning Brooke's body. His name was George, and he gave me a more forceful handshake than I thought was necessary.

"Fantastic plans," George said. "Thank you so much for your generosity, Brooke! We couldn't have done it without you."

Brooke managed to pull me away, and we finally stood in front of the large display. Boards with architectural plans were set up on easels as well as pieces of fabric and carpet samples. I couldn't really picture what it would look like, so I watched Brooke as she studied the display. She got close to the architectural plans, squinting and reading the details. She paused at the fabric samples and nodded approvingly.

"What do you think?" I asked.

"I like the plans. The restored crown moldings will really give the room a sense of grandeur, and I like the fabric they've chosen for the window treatments and the chairs. The colors are fresh and modern, but the designs are period appropriate. What do you think?"

"Looks good, I guess. I'll have to see it when it's finished."

"They'll throw a party once it's complete," she said. "I can probably get tickets." She turned and met my eyes, her right eyebrow arching. My skin heated, since all I could think about was touching her soft skin.

"Yeah," I said. "Sure."

People were crowding around us, trying to get a better look at the displays. I put my arm out to block a woman from pressing against Brooke.

"Here, get behind me," I said. "I'll make a path."

Turning to make my way through the crowd, Brooke touched my back and followed. I moved toward the edge of the room, relieved to get some space.

"Follow me," Brooke said. "There's a balcony out here."

She led me to a tall set of glass doors flanked by enormous gold curtains. I had the feeling we shouldn't be doing this, but I glanced behind me, and no one was looking. I followed her out the glass door and closed it behind me.

FOUR

When I reached the balcony, I was surprised to see the edge of the park behind the hotel. It was dark now, but several ornate lamps lit a path to the park. The air was cool, and stars were visible in the sky.

"I never realized there was a balcony back here."

"Great view of the park, especially in the daytime," Brooke said. "The cool air feels nice."

She turned to face me, and I took in the shape of her mouth, her full lips, and the curve of her chin. She stepped closer, and I felt a puff of her breath on my chin.

"Thanks for coming with me tonight," she said.

"No problem. I wanted to get to know you better."

Her breath hitched. I took a step closer and rubbed my thumb over her cheek. It was softer than silk. I wet my lips, wanting to kiss her so badly, my chest ached.

Why did she ask me to go out with her? Women like this never gave me a second glance. I was invisible to the residents of the building, most of them not even offering a thanks if I held a door open for them.

"Brooke..." I said.

She lifted her face to mine.

"Kiss me, Evan."

I cupped her face with my hands and leaned in. Her lips brushed mine, tentatively at first, then with more pressure. Her arms slid around my waist, and her lips parted a little.

Her mouth was hot and soft. She sucked on my lower lip, and I let out a moan. She made a noise in the back of her throat, then surprised me by sliding her hands over the back of my pants and cupping my ass.

Blood rushed to my cock. Damn, I missed having a woman grab me like that. I deepened the kiss, pressing my tongue against hers, tasting her and breathing in her scent. The sounds of the party faded, and I forgot where we were.

The balcony doorknob rattled, and the door opened. Brooke quickly released me.

"Oh, I'm sorry," a man said. "I didn't realize anyone was out here."

"It's fine," Brooke said.

She was suddenly standing several feet away from me, as if she didn't have her hands full of my ass cheeks seconds earlier. The door opened and four people filed out to the balcony, chattering and laughing.

I stuck my hands in my pockets and grinned.

"Sorry," she said. "I got carried away."

"I'm not sorry," I said.

Seconds passed where she looked into my eyes, and a smile quirked her lips.

"Let's go back inside," she said. "There's one more person I need to see, then we'll get a drink you'll like."

"Sure."

I let her go first and tried to calm my breathing from our hot and heavy kiss. She opened the door, and we worked our way through the room. The crowd had dispersed a little, filling the hallway outside the reception room.

"There she is," Brooke said.

"Who?"

"My boss. The short woman in red."

I looked around and saw her. "Got it."

Make sure the boss sees you, then duck out. I understood. The woman made her way toward us, and Brooke put herself directly in her path.

"Diane," Brooke said. "Good to see you."

Diane was holding a glass of champagne. "Brooke, nice to see you. Have you seen the plans? They're ready to start now, thanks to you."

I glanced at Brooke, but her face gave nothing away. "I was happy to help. This is my friend, Evan."

Friend? Okay.

I offered my hand, and Diane gave it a little shake.

"Lovely to meet you. Would you like some champagne, Evan?"

"We already had some, but we need to get going," Brooke said.

"Oh, alright. See you tomorrow."

I was relieved when she grabbed my hand and led me out to the cooler hallway.

"Well, that was interesting," I said.

"Go ahead, say it. It was boring."

"Yeah, a place like this isn't my typical hangout."

We reached the main lobby, but instead of turning left toward the exit, she turned a sharp right.

"This way," she said. "I'll buy you a beer."

I walked beside her down a narrow hallway with plush green carpeting. We took a right, then a left, then...

"Wow," I said.

We came to a low-ceilinged room with a long mahogany bar and a man playing the piano in the corner. A few patrons sat at the bar, drinking tall glasses of beer. They glanced appreciatively at Brooke.

"Hey, Charlie," she said to the bartender.

"Brooke." His brown hair was threaded with gray, and he wore a black shirt and pants. His rolled-up sleeves showed off heavily tattooed forearms. "Want your usual?"

"Two," she said, leading me to a table in the corner.

After pulling out a chair for her, I sat down and took in the dark paneled walls, textured blue wallpaper, and the scarred but heavily polished table. The floors were clean, not sticky like Cooper's.

"I had no idea there was a bar back here," I said.

"They just renovated it. They refinished the woodwork and had the original wallpaper reproduced by a company in New York..." She shook her head. "There I go, boring you again."

"No way. I like old buildings, too. Wish I worked in one. I don't care for modern buildings as much." I realized what I said and mentally kicked myself. "Well, the building where you live is okay, I just—"

"No, say what you mean. You prefer older buildings."

Charlie came over with our drinks. "Here ya go."

"Thanks, Charlie."

"No problem, Brooke." His dark eyes scanned my face, my shirt, and my blazer. I had the feeling I was being sized up. "Just holler if you need anything."

He left, and I wondered if I was reading too much into his once-over. The beer was ice cold, and I couldn't wait to drink it. I held it up high, ready to make a toast. Brooke held her glass up.

"To old buildings and new friendships," I said.

Brooke smiled, and it lit up her whole face. She was beautiful, radiant, so intelligent—and I had no idea what the hell she was doing with a guy like me.

I took a long sip and swallowed. "Damn, this is good. What is it?"

"It's from the brewery in Carlton. It's my favorite."

I took in her blue tailored suit and jewelry while she drank. She gave her bottom lip a small lick to remove the beer foam, and my skin tingled with awareness.

"Seems like you're a regular here."

She looked away for a second, then nodded. "I used to be."

"You know the bartender."

Her eyes met mine. "Yes, he's a good friend of mine."

I considered that and took another sip. There was more to that story.

"So, you like craft beer?" she asked.

"Yeah, I like to try different kinds."

"Do you drink much?" she asked.

"Nah, not really. Maybe a beer with dinner at the bar, or at a game with my buddies. I don't get drunk any more. Too old for that shit."

"Oh, come on," she said. "How old are you, twenty-five?"

"I'm twenty-seven," I said. "Why, how old are you?"

Damn, there I go again, saying something stupid.

"I'm sorry, it's rude to ask."

Her laugh was husky, and it made me smile.

"It's okay. I'm thirty-four," she said. "I just had a birthday last week."

"Thirty-four? I never woulda guessed."

She leaned a little closer. "You're good for my ego."

I took another sip, wondering just where this was going. Tapping her fingers on the scarred table, she looked at my hands, then her gaze traveled up my arms. She wet her lips a little. A zing went through me, and I wanted to kiss her again, to finish what we started on that balcony—preferably near a bed.

"Evan," she said. "I have a proposal for you. I hope you'll keep an open mind."

That's not what I was expecting to hear.

I placed my glass on the table, waiting to hear what kind of proposal a woman like this could have for a guy like me.

FIVE

"Okay," I said. "What is it?"

The guy playing the piano stopped, and the bar went silent a few seconds. The few patrons applauded, and he got up and went to the bar.

Brooke sat up a little straighter. "I'd like to propose a business arrangement. I need a companion for some upcoming business events. Things like tonight, cocktail parties, maybe a few charity events."

I blinked. "But why do you need me? You could get any guy you want. Hell, ask Charlie."

"No, Charlie wouldn't want to. Plus, I need someone who's available weekends."

I grinned. "How do you know what I'm up to? I could be busy weekends."

"Well, what do you do on the weekend?"

"Let's see." I drummed my fingers on the table. "I do laundry, hang out with Liam and the guys at Cooper's…"

I knew my list sounded lame.

"Sometimes I pick up extra work with one of the guys from Cooper's, but I haven't done that in a while. If the roofers or drywall guys need an extra set of hands, sometimes they'll pay me under the table to work with them on the weekend. I'm saving up for..."

For what? A run-down house on the wrong side of the tracks? A house that needed thousands of dollars in renovations I couldn't afford? I was handy, but new wiring, plumbing, and heating systems cost a shitload of money.

"Saving for what?" Brooke asked.

"I'm saving up for a house, remember?"

"That's right."

She clasped her hands, and I looked down at them—long, delicate fingers with perfectly shaped fingernails coated in a clear polish, a delicate gold bracelet sparkling on her wrist, and a ring with a red stone. I was suddenly self-conscious about my own rough hands.

"I think it's wonderful that you're saving for a house. I can help you with that."

"Yeah, you gave me your card. I'm not ready yet."

She shifted in her seat. The piano playing started up again, this time with a ballad. Brooke cleared her throat.

"I'd like to pay you to be my companion. I'd like you to be on call for any engagements that might pop up the next two weeks. Are you interested?"

"Wait a second." I put my hand up. "You want to pay me?"

She gave me a dazzling smile, one that said she knew exactly what she was doing.

"Yes."

"How much?" I asked.

She took a sip of beer, and the seconds ticked by slowly. She put her glass down.

"Name your price," she said.

I searched her face for a hint of a smile, but there was nothing. Her blue eyes met mine, and suddenly I wanted to kiss her again, to feel her body against mine.

"Dance with me," I said, putting out my hand.

"What?"

I shoved my chair back and stood. "Dance with me, Miss Fancy Pants, and we'll talk terms."

Her nostrils flared, and her cheeks flushed. The piano player went into a second ballad, and she rose to her feet. Taking her hand, I led her to an open spot on the floor and pulled her close. I took her left hand in my right and swirled her around.

Brooke laughed, and the sound made my heart squeeze in my chest.

"Wow," she said. "You know how to dance!"

"Surprised?" I asked.

"A little. Where did you learn to dance?"

She moved closer, her clothes brushing against mine. I inhaled her flowery perfume.

"I'm not a caveman," I said. "I know how to dance with a woman."

We swayed to the music, and her body relaxed a little more. I studied her face—her dark eyelashes, nice skin, and those lips... Now I knew how soft they were and how good they felt, I wanted to feel them again.

"I know how to tie a Windsor knot in a tie, too."

"Yes, you'll do nicely."

I wasn't sure what she meant by that, but I liked the way her body was pressing against mine.

"You really gonna pay me to be your date?" I asked.

"Yes. I said before, name your price."

I looked away for a few seconds, considering. How much to be at her beck and call for a couple of weeks? I thought about the balance in my savings account. She was loaded. I thought about her high-end condo unit. I saw her in the parking lot once, getting into a pricey sedan.

I decided to go for broke.

"You couldn't afford me," I said.

She grinned. "Try me."

I twirled her again, then pulled her close. "Be on call for dinners, parties, nights and weekends for the next two weeks?"

"Yes. It might require some travel and late nights. Some overnights, perhaps."

Wow, overnights.

Heat zinged to my groin. I could deal with a few more ritzy parties if it meant adding to my savings account and spending the night with a beautiful woman.

"I work Monday through Friday, seven-thirty until four or so."

"I wouldn't need your services during your regular work hours," she said. "I'm usually working during those hours as well."

I wet my lips. I had to play this right. I couldn't ask for too little, or too much, but what was too much for a woman like this?

I decided I could use another five grand. That would put my savings in a much better place. Ten thousand more, and I could afford a down payment and some renovations.

"Ten thousand," I said firmly.

She didn't flinch or give away what she was thinking.

"Done," she said. "But for that price, I'll definitely need some overnights."

Heat rushed over my body, making my pulse pound and my cock throb. I wanted this woman. I wondered if her sexiness extended to the bedroom.

Our dancing slowed, then stopped. I lifted her chin and kissed her, a soft press of lips, a quick reminder of our earlier kiss on the balcony. She sighed and pressed the tip of her tongue against mine. I'd just started to deepen the kiss when I heard a small cough.

We looked up to find the bartender standing a few feet away, brows furrowed, big hands on his hips.

"Everything okay, Brooke?"

"Yeah, Charlie. Everything's fine."

He gave me a withering stare, then slowly turned and walked away.

"What the hell was that about?" I asked.

"Oh, nothing." She waved her hand and laughed again, but this laugh sounded forced. "He's just a bit protective of me."

"Okay..." I said.

"We never dated, it's nothing like that."

"None of my business," I said.

The piano music changed to an upbeat song as the bar filled up with chatting people.

"You finished with your beer?" I asked.

"Yes. I'll just get my purse—"

I was already pulling my wallet out of my back pocket. "No, when you're with me, I pay."

"Alright."

She picked up her purse and waited. Thankfully Charlie had dropped off a bill on our table. My eyes nearly popped out of my head at the cost of the beers. I pulled out enough bills for the beers and a tip and left it on the table.

Making our way through the bar, I looked up and caught Charlie's eye on the way out. He gave me a small nod. We walked through the maze of hallways, past the front desk, and reached the glass entry doors. I held one open for Brooke, and soon we were out in the cool night air.

"Where's your car?" I asked.

"This way," she said, walking in the opposite direction from my truck.

We walked slowly, my mind spinning with the possibilities. Just a couple of weeks squiring this beautiful woman around, and I could start looking for a house. I couldn't wait to tell Liam.

"Thanks for coming with me tonight," she said.

"No problem. It was interesting."

She stopped. "It's going to get a lot more interesting over the next two weeks."

She dug in her purse and pulled out some keys.

"Is this where I give you a polite kiss goodnight?" I asked.

Half her face was in shadow, and the other half was lit by a streetlight. I admired the slant of her high cheekbones and the full bow of her top lip. Putting my hand on her waist, I waited for permission to kiss her again.

She reached up and slid her warm hand around the back of my neck, pulling me down. Our lips met softly at first, then a little more urgently. Before I could deepen the kiss, she pulled away.

"Any chance our overnights could start tonight?" I asked.

"Can't," she said. "Have a very early meeting tomorrow."

"Oh," I said, unable to hide my disappointment.

"You'll hear from me soon." She winked, then walked around to the driver's side of her car. "Have a good night, Evan."

The automatic door locks clicked open, and she opened the door and climbed inside. She started the car, turned on the headlights, and drove off.

I turned and walked back to my truck with ten thousand reasons to be happy.

SIX

"Ten thousand dollars?" Liam asked. "Are you crazy? No, wait, is *she* crazy?"

Liam sat across the kitchen table, his fork in midair, a piece of pancake drooping from his fork.

"A little louder, Liam, I don't think all the neighbors heard."

"You shoulda asked for twenty! She can afford it."

"I thought ten was pushing it," I said. "I only need five. Ten gives me some extra padding for repairs and stuff. I'm still gonna end up with a fixer-upper."

Liam stuffed the pancake bite into his mouth and chewed furiously. He swallowed and leaned forward.

"She wants you to go to parties and to...service her?" He smirked. "Shit, you have all the luck. First, you get this job, then this chick wants you to be her..."

"Date."

"Gigolo," Liam said, smirking. "Damn! Wait'll I tell the guys at Cooper's!"

I dropped my fork, and it clattered on my plate. "Liam, you can't tell the guys about this. Please!"

He let out a long sigh and busied himself cutting up more of his pancakes.

"Don't fuck this up for me. This is my chance to get the rest of the money together faster and help Matty."

Liam sighed. "Does it suck that much?"

"Does what suck?"

"Living here. With me." He gave me his lopsided grin.

"No, dumbass, it doesn't suck. But I'll miss hearing you sing off-key in the shower every morning."

"Fuck you," he said, grinning.

"I'm not going anywhere just yet," I said. "Gotta find a house first."

"You've been looking, though," he said. "Online, right?"

"Yeah."

"Well, have her show you some houses. She knows the area really well, right?"

I picked up the bottle of syrup and poured more on my pancakes. "I guess."

"You guess? What aren't you telling me?"

"She doesn't sell shitty little houses I can afford, remember? She sells mansions. Big fuckin' houses with seven bedrooms and three-car garages. That's how she makes her money."

"Yeah, I know. And that's how she affords a *gigolo*."

I balled up my napkin and tossed it at his face. It hit him on the chin, then fell onto his plate.

"Damnit! That's my breakfast!"

"You deserved it." I took my last few bites and scraped my chair back. "We gotta get going. Traffic's been awful with the spring road construction."

I brought my plate and mug to the counter, loaded my dishes into the dishwasher, and Liam did the same. He could be a pain in the ass, but we made a good team. He had my back for the last several years. Between parties, watching sports on TV, and hanging out at Cooper's, he was always around.

I was looking forward to buying a house, but it would be sad to move away from Liam. Stepping into my work boots, I started tying them.

"So, tell me something," Liam said as he put on his Red Sox hat. "She got any friends who need to hire a gigolo?"

I reached over and snatched the hat from his head.

"Give it back!"

But I threw my arm around his neck and put him into a headlock.

"Take it back!" I taunted him.

He struggled in my grip and muttered something.

"What?" I asked, loosening my grip.

"I said, I'm sorry I'm not a gigolo, too."

"Jerk," I said. "I gotta get to work, but I'll kick your ass at darts later."

Besides our group dart tournaments, Liam and I had a long-running competition going. Liam had won a hundred and seventy-five games, and I'd won a hundred seventy-seven. He was slightly better than me, so I loved being ahead of him. The loser had to pay for the night's drinks.

Liam gave me shit all the way out to my truck, and I gave it right back.

* * *

THE DAY WAS A BUSY ONE. I replaced several light bulbs in the stairway and storage areas and mopped the tile floor in the lobby, keeping an eye out for Brooke. Several tenants and visitors came and went, and none of them looked me in the eye. I was part of the woodwork to these people, which is partly why Brooke stood out to me—she looked at me and smiled.

Well, her killer curves didn't hurt one bit, either.

A tall man in a suit walked through the lobby, talking on his phone.

"I don't care," he said. "Add another seventy thousand to the offer. That's chump change."

He got on the elevator, still arguing with the person on the other end of the phone.

Chump change—I shook my head. I didn't even make that much in a year. What would it be like, I wondered, to be so cavalier with money?

I finished mopping and looked around the lobby to admire my work. Mopping the lobby was satisfying, even though it would get dusty from foot traffic by the end of the day.

I was sitting in the break room for lunch when my phone buzzed with a text. My heart leaped when I saw it was from Brooke.

Can you come by my unit? I have something to give you.

I looked at my watch. I had enough time. Riding the elevator to her floor, I wondered what she wanted. Thankfully, her hallway was empty. I didn't want anyone to see me going in without a ladder or a tool belt. I knocked on her door and heard heels clicking, and the door swung open.

"Come in, Evan," she said, looking gorgeous in a blue knee-length dress that showed off every curve.

"Hey," I said, closing the door behind me. "You look great."

It was exactly the right thing to say. She smiled.

"Thank you."

"You wanted to see me?" I stuffed my hands into my pockets, suddenly feeling awkward. "I only have a few minutes."

"Of course." She picked up an envelope from the counter and handed it to me.

"What's this?"

"Money," she said simply. "You need more dressy clothing

for the next two weeks. Buy some pants and blazers, shoes, and you'll need a suit and some ties."

The envelope was open, so I peeked inside. There was a thick stack of hundreds.

"Brooke, this is way too much."

"No, it isn't. You'll be going to Blaine's Apparel downtown. You know where that is?"

I nodded. Blaine's Apparel was an expensive men's clothing store. I knew exactly where it was, even though I never set foot in the place.

"I can go later when I get off work."

"Good. And I wanted to talk to you about our sleeping arrangements."

My cock twitched. *Now* we were talking.

"What do you have in mind?"

"Are you still interested in sleeping over?" Her dark eyebrow arched, and my skin heated.

"Yes."

"I was thinking...it's probably not a great idea for you to come and go from this condo every day."

Shit, I didn't think of that. "That's true."

"I've arranged for a suite at the Carlisle for two weeks. It's perfect timing since I'm having new carpet installed in my bedrooms."

"But...isn't that expensive?" I asked, mentally calculating the cost of a room there, never mind a suite.

"It's perfectly fine. It's just for a short time, and you won't be seen coming and going at all hours."

"Yeah, you're probably right." I folded the envelope and stuffed it into my back pocket.

"I'll need your services tomorrow night. It's a little get together at my boss' house. I'll text you the address."

"Right."

I wanted so badly to touch her, but she looked so clean and unwrinkled. I probably had dust on my uniform from mopping and working in the grimy supply closet.

Heat and electricity arced between us. I took a step closer, my gaze focusing on the perfect bow of her upper lip.

"I want to kiss you right now, but I won't," I said. "Not on the clock."

I lifted my right hand—I'd washed my hands before I came up—and brushed her hair behind her ear. She sucked in a breath, and I caught a hint of her perfume. I leaned forward, so my mouth was by her ear.

"And I intend to find out what you wear beneath your clothes," I murmured. I started to move away, but she put her hands on my shoulders.

"I was hoping for a quick kiss." She was breathing faster now, and her lashes fluttered—she was damn near swooning.

"I don't want to mess up your lipstick...yet."

A needy moan slipped out of her mouth. Slipping out of her grasp, I headed for the door before an embarrassing bulge grew in my pants. I looked over my shoulder as I left.

"Gotta run."

She grasped the kitchen counter like she needed to steady herself.

The door clicked shut behind me as I walked to the elevator, chuckling like a fool.

SEVEN

After work, I drove downtown to the suit shop. Opening the door, a bell tinkled to announce my presence. I looked around and immediately regretted coming here in my work shirt and pants.

The place looked high end with gleaming wood floors, nice lighting, and several mannequins dressed in suits. I felt self-conscious about the name tag on my shirt. An older man in a dark suit and red tie approached.

"Can I help you?" he asked, looking me over. His gaze stopped on my name tag.

"Yes, I need to get measured for a suit."

He frowned. "I don't think we have anything in your style."

I paused, a ball of dread forming in my stomach. This guy was gonna give me a hard time, but I wasn't having it. I took a few more steps and looked at a mannequin.

"How about this suit?" I asked.

The door tinkled, and another man came in. He was wearing dressy pants, a button-down shirt, and a tie. The salesman straightened his tie.

"I don't think that particular suit is for you. It's quite pricey.

Excuse me." He walked over to the other customer. "Can I help you, sir?"

My hands tightened into fists. I looked around the store but saw no one else.

Fuck this place! I didn't want to spend Brooke's money with this asshole. I yanked open the door and walked out, storming up the sidewalk just to get away. I kept walking past the other shops without a destination in mind.

I must have looked furious, because a woman walking a small dog made a wide circle when passing me. I unclenched my fists and tried to relax my jaw, but kept walking for several minutes.

I passed a vendor selling hot pretzels out of a cart. A dad and a small boy were buying pretzels. Long shadows from the buildings shaded the sidewalk in the late afternoon sun as a group of giggling teenaged girls passed me. I saw a sign for Spring Street, and it jogged something in my memory.

Brooke. I stopped and pulled out my wallet, pawing through the discount cards until I found the business card I was looking for.

Brooke Sinclair
Turner Real Estate
45 Spring Street

That's where I'd seen Spring Street. I stuffed her card back in my wallet and turned down Spring Street. It was a quieter street off Main with sidewalks on just one side. I passed an art shop and an antique shop with a big banner announcing SALE TODAY!

The buildings a little further down were smaller. I saw twenty-five on a building and kept walking. A large brick home held a dental office. There were several Victorian homes next.

Large and ornate, they had wide wraparound front porches, and one had a turret with curved windows.

Stopping in front of a dark green house with the number forty-five, I climbed the front stairs and saw a small sign near the door.

First & Second floor - Turner Real Estate
Third Floor - Murphy & Cahill Law Office

I paused. Why the hell was I here? To tell Brooke I'd been treated like a second-class citizen in the suit shop? I almost wanted to give her the money back, tell her I'd changed my mind, but I thought about Matty and sighed. I wished for a stable home for me and Matty—a home that was calm and free of stress and tension.

I opened the front door. The inside was cool, and the floor was covered in thick maroon carpeting. There was a staircase to my right, and to my left was a woman sitting at a desk, wearing glasses and typing on a computer keyboard. She looked up and smiled when I approached.

"Can I help you?"

Her blonde hair was pulled back into a sleek ponytail, and her face looked friendly.

"Yes, I'm looking for Brooke. Is this her office?"

"It is, but she's out at a showing. Would you like to make an appointment?"

"No," I said. "I'll just give her a call. Thanks."

I turned to leave, heading toward the door when she spoke again.

"You're Evan, aren't you?"

I turned around and looked at her. "Yeah, how'd you know?"

"The name tag, and...she told me about you."

Oh, damn. "Brooke told you about me?"

She nodded and stood. "I'm Julia, her assistant."

I walked back and held out my hand. She gave it a girlish squeeze.

"What, uh...what did she say about me?"

Up close, Julia looked very young. Her face was unlined, and she had a cluster of freckles on her nose and cheeks.

"Brooke said you were a friend who'd be escorting her to some upcoming events." Julia smiled and pushed her glasses up her nose. "She didn't say you'd be stopping by today."

Friend, huh? I searched Julia's face for judgment, but I didn't see any.

"Yeah, I was just walking down Main Street when I noticed Spring Street..." I stuffed my hands into my pockets. "Listen, do you know any place I can get a suit?"

"Did you go to Blaine's Apparel ? They have the best suits in the area."

"Yeah. I went. And I left. They were ass... they were rude. The guy walked right past me and helped another customer."

Julia's eyes widened. "Really? That's unusual. The shop usually gives top-notch customer service."

"I went in there with plenty of cash. They just never gave me a chance."

Julia considered that for a second. She took her glasses off and looked me up and down.

"It's four-thirty. I know Blaine's stays open until six on weekdays. Just give me five minutes to close up, and we'll go back together."

"You don't have to do that."

She held her hand up. "Brooke would want me to help you with this. I don't mind closing early. I'll just forward the phone to my cell. I'll be ready to go in just a minute."

"Okay."

I wasn't a fan of going back to that shop, Julia woman seemed sure she could help me. I stuck my hands in my pockets and looked around the entry. There was an oval decorative mirror on the wall, and beside an oval mirror were plaques listing Top Selling Agent of the Year. I noticed Brooke's name listed as the top-selling agent for the last five years.

I made a mental note to razz her about it, then spotted another row of plaques for Outstanding Customer Service and Agent of the Year. Again, Brooke's name was listed several times.

Julia turned off her computer and stuffed some folders in a drawer. She picked up a purse and walked over to me.

"Brooke wins a lot of these awards, huh?"

"Oh yes," Julia said. "She's on track to win the top sales award for this year, too."

I grinned. "Bet she was the teacher's pet in school."

"She was in the top five percent of her class at grad school."

Grad school. I had taken a few classes at the local community college, but I never finished because I ran out of money. I was so proud of Matty for doing what I couldn't.

I followed Julia out the door into the bright sunlight. I blinked in the glare, suddenly remembering I'd walked from the suit shop.

"Listen," I said. "I'm parked down by the suit shop. I walked here."

Julia withdrew a giant pair of sunglasses and put them on, shielding her eyes.

"That's fine, we can walk. It's a nice day."

I peered at her tall heels, wondering how she'd maneuver the bumpy downtown sidewalks, but she hitched her bag over her shoulder and started walking. We didn't speak as we walked down the quiet street. I felt out of place walking beside her in my work uniform and scuffed work boots.

"How long have you known Brooke?" I asked.

"Seven years."

A man in a suit walked toward us. He glanced at me, then his gaze slowly scanned Julia. When we passed, he gave her a wide smile, but she ignored him.

"So...Brooke told you about me?"

Her lips quirked. "Yes, she did."

We both dodged around a dog on a leash sniffing the sidewalk. I waited for her to add more, but she didn't.

"Like what?"

"Evan Handler. Twenty-seven years old. Lives at an apartment on Western Avenue with roommate Liam McKenzie. One younger brother, Matthew, currently at the University of Vermont. No arrests. One parking ticket. Currently employed as a maintenance worker at one-sixty Brookdale Avenue."

I stopped in the middle of the sidewalk and stared at her. She stopped and let out a long sigh and took off her sunglasses.

"Evan. Did you really think that Brooke wouldn't check into you before your arrangement?"

My face heated. "Well... I..."

Julia put her sunglasses back on and started walking briskly. I had to jog a few steps to catch up.

"Brooke Sinclair is a very busy woman. I had to check into your background to make sure you were...appropriate. Her upcoming engagements are very important."

I considered this and wondered why she chose me, instead of hitting up some rich dude who probably owned several suits. Julia's phone rang, and she fished it out of her bag.

"Hello? Hi. Listen, I can't talk right now. I'm right in the middle of something. I'll call you later. Yes. Yes. Okay."

She hung up as we walked up to the door of the suit shop. I opened the door, and we both stepped inside. The same jerk came gliding over to us, completely ignoring me, but smiling broadly for Julia.

"Can I help you, miss?"

"I need to speak to the owner."

The man's smile dropped from his face. "Mr. Blaine is very busy right now, Miss. Can I help you with something?"

Julia frowned. "I need to speak to him right away. Tell him it's Julia Nichols from Turner Real Estate."

The man scurried off. A few other customers milled around. Heaviness lodged in my gut like I'd swallowed a rock. I grew up pretty broke and knew the routine in a place like this. These sales guys were always going to look down their noses at me.

"Listen, isn't there somewhere else we can go?" I asked.

"No, I'll take care of this."

A tall man in a brown suit came over. "How can I help you, miss?"

Julia touched my arm. "This man came into your shop a short time ago and your salesman refused to help him."

"I'm so sorry, Miss...?"

"Julia Nichols. I'm Brooke Sinclair's assistant."

His eyes raked me over, then he plastered on a smile that was a bit too wide.

"My apologies," he said. "We'll take care of this right away. Follow me."

We followed him across the store to a pair of dressing rooms. He signaled to another salesman, who came over with a tape measure. Julia sat in a chair by a tall mirror and checked her phone.

"Stand up straight and relax your shoulders, please," the man said.

I endured the measuring tape being tugged all over my body. Julia's phone rang again.

"Turner Real Estate, how can I help you?" she said. "No,

I'm sorry, she's not here at the moment, can I take a message?" She took out a small notebook and a pen and took a message.

The salesman brought me over to a rack of shirts, asking what material I liked. I touched the shirts, each one softer than the next. I was terrible at picking out colors.

"How about white?" I asked.

"Sure. Can I recommend this blue as well?"

He took out a blue shirt and held it up to me.

"Okay," I said, grateful he didn't select a pink one. I'd seen guys wear pink dress shirts, but I wasn't sure I could pull it off.

"I have a few different jackets I'd like you to try on."

He carried some clothes into a changing room and left so I could try things on. I tried on a dark grey suit with a white shirt first. When I came out of the dressing room, Julia was off the phone.

"Oh, nice!" she said approvingly. "Jacket arms are a little long."

"We can take the sleeves up," the salesman said.

I held still while he marked the sleeve with pins.

"Why don't you try on the navy jacket, Mr. Handler? I'd like to see how that one looks on you."

"Okay," I said, glancing at Julia.

She grinned and looked back down at her phone. I strode into the waiting room smiling. I wasn't used to being called Mr. Handler.

I tried on a few more jackets and pants. Julia gave me a thumbs-up, and shook her head a couple of times. In total, I chose a dark grey suit, the navy suit, four shirts, and four ties.

"Excellent," Julia said.

At the register, I was relieved to have enough cash to pay the total. I had to leave the suits since the pants and jacket sleeves had to be hemmed, but left carrying a bag with the shirts and ties.

We left the store, and Julia slipped on her sunglasses again.

"Thanks, Julia," I said. "I really appreciate it."

"Glad to help. Let me give you my card, just in case you need anything else."

She dug a card out of her purse and handed it to me. I stuffed it into my shirt pocket.

"Do you need a ride back?"

"No, thank you," she said. "I'll be fine. Have a good evening, Evan."

"You, too."

I walked back to my truck, wondering just what the hell I'd gotten myself into.

EIGHT

It was three o'clock the next day before my phone buzzed with a text from Brooke.

Can you pick me up at 6:30 at the hotel tonight?

I had impure thoughts about what she'd look like beneath her dressy clothes. I was willing to bet money she wore sexy underthings—lacy and see-through, soft in my hands. Almost as soft as her skin.

I shook my head to clear my thoughts and quickly texted back that I'd pick her up at six-thirty.

Grabbing my ladder, I headed to the elevator to fix a light on the third floor. The short ladder I needed was hanging by a hook on the back wall of the supply room. I carried it down the hall to the elevator. Mrs. Wilson, an old woman who lived on three, was trying to push the elevator button while juggling some shopping bags.

"I can help you with that, Mrs. Wilson."

She looked up at me and grinned. "Oh, thank you, dear."

I pushed the button, then grabbed a few of her shopping bags with my free hand. When the elevator door opened, we went inside.

"I live on the third floor, dearie."

"I know, I've helped you with your bags before."

She patted my arm. "Oh, that's right. I remember now. How's your wife?"

"I'm not married, Mrs. Wilson."

"Oh, I'm sorry. I must have you confused with someone else."

"That's okay."

We rode the elevator up. When it reached the third floor, I left my ladder in the hall beside the elevator and brought Mrs. Wilson's groceries to her door.

She tried to press some bills into my hand, but I shook my head.

"We're not allowed to accept tips."

"Oh, alright. Thank you, then."

I checked the hall light that was reported to be blinking on and off. Taking off the glass cover, I checked the wires and connections. One of the wires was loose, and one of the bulbs had a crack in it. After going into a supply closet for tools and a bulb, I fixed it and went back downstairs to drop off the ladder.

The lobby was quiet except for a man in a pin-striped suit and shiny black shoes, pacing back and forth and muttering. When he heard my footsteps approach, he looked up.

"You," he said, snapping his fingers. "You, there."

I bristled, since I hated when someone snapped their fingers at me.

I pointed to the name tag on my shirt. "I'm Evan."

"Yeah, whatever. I'm looking for a package. Where do you put packages when they're delivered?"

"I work in maintenance, I don't deal with packages," I said, trying to keep contempt out of my voice. "Why don't you—"

"Jesus, everyone here is incompetent. Incompetent!"

Oh, this was rich. He paced back and forth again. I crossed my arms and sighed.

"I was about to say, why don't you check at the desk with Carly? She's the one who holds packages."

"I was just *at* the desk, and no one was there."

That was odd. Frowning, I walked toward the desk area, which was behind a partition. Carly was standing there, talking on the phone. She smiled and wiggled her fingers at me. I walked back toward the asshole.

"Well, she's there now."

"Oh, great," he said. "Finally."

He stalked off toward the desk, but I hovered, waiting to see how he acted with Carly. She greeted him, and he asked for his package. She found it and handed it over. He took it and stalked out of the building. I went over to the desk.

"Carly, you okay?" I asked.

"Yes," she sighed. "What an asshole."

"What's his name? I think he lives on six."

She ran her hand through her curly brown hair. "His name is Brad Jacobs. I went to grab something in the supply closet for thirty seconds, and I must have missed him. He's always like that."

"I'll steer clear of him. There's no need to act like that."

"Right?" she said. "I hate it when they treat us like their servants."

"No kidding. Gotta get back to work."

"Talk to you later, Evan."

I started walking away, then I thought of something and turned around.

"Carly, can I ask you something?"

"Sure."

I felt a little silly, but I needed a woman's perspective.

"I'm going out with my... girlfriend tonight. We're going to her boss' house for dinner."

"Ew," Carly said, wrinkling her nose.

"Yeah, not my idea of fun. Should I bring something?"

"Yes, definitely bring something. A bottle of wine? Flowers are always nice."

"Okay, thanks, Carly."

The rest of the day passed quickly, and I forgot about the asshole in the pin-striped suit. After work, I stopped by the grocery store to check out flowers. There were so many kinds, I didn't know what to choose. I reached for a bunch, but I hesitated. Would they be able to tell I bought them at a grocery store? Probably not.

I chose a colorful bouquet with pink, yellow, and purple flowers and started to walk away. What about Brooke? I didn't want to show up with flowers for someone else and not have any flowers for her.

Damn.

I turned back, grabbed a second bouquet, and took them up to the register.

When I got home, I killed some time until taking a shower. I put on my dress pants and one of my new shirts. Liam texted that he'd gone with some of the guys to Cooper's. I smiled, knowing I was missing out on some fun with the guys, but a job was a job.

Besides, I was looking forward to getting to know Brooke more.

* * *

BROOKE HAD SENT me her floor and room number, so when I got to the hotel, I headed to the elevator. I went up to the fifth floor, shifting from foot to foot.

When the elevator doors opened, I stepped into the hall and found Brooke's door. My heartbeat sped up as I knocked. A few seconds later, Brooke opened the door.

"Hi," she said.

I stepped in and handed her the flowers. "Hey. You look beautiful."

"Thank you."

Lifting the flowers to her nose, she breathed in deep. She wore a short-sleeved black dress that hugged her curves and stopped just above her knees.

"Thanks for the flowers. I haven't gotten flowers in a long time."

"That's a shame."

She stepped to the small kitchen area, opened a cupboard, and took out a tall glass.

I looked around the suite while she filled the glass with water. A laptop sat on a small table with two chairs. The living room had a couch and chairs, covered in dark fabric that looked expensive. Two paintings hung on the wall above the couch. A closed door led to what I assumed was the bedroom.

"This is really nice," I said, wondering just how much a suite like this cost.

Brooke came over to me, looking me up and down.

"Very handsome."

Pulling her close, I put my arms around her waist. She smiled and looked up at me.

"You seem shorter today," I said.

She laughed. "That's because I don't have my heels on."

I looked down at her bare feet. Her toenails were painted pink. I loved how small she felt, resting her hand on my chest. The top of her head was just below my nose. Her dress was soft, and I could feel the warmth of her skin beneath the fabric. I pulled her tight against me, enjoying the sensation of her body against mine. Bending over, I caught a whiff of her flowery scent and pressed my lips to hers.

Her arms slid around my neck as we had some unhurried kisses. Finally, no interruptions. Brooke sighed into my mouth.

The tip of her tongue touched mine, sending a jolt through every nerve ending in my body. She took a halting step back, and I went with her until her hip banged into a chair.

"Oh!" she said.

"Sorry. Got a little too enthusiastic."

I released her, and she smoothed the fabric on her dress.

"I'd really like to continue this," she said. "But we really need to get to this dinner."

"Sure. This is all new to me. I'm not really sure what to do."

"I understand. Just so you know, I've never done this, either. Hired a... hired a man to come to events with me."

"Yeah, I was wondering why you hired me. You could get a guy that was a lawyer or someone brainy like that. Someone with a better job. Why me?"

"Well, I like you, and you don't have to be a lawyer to be smart. I can tell you're smart, Evan. And I don't need any romantic drama the next couple of weeks."

My stomach sank. Maybe I was reading too much into her glances, her kisses. She saw this as a business transaction—period. I could get behind that.

"Right, got it. Let's head out. My truck is parked on the street outside, it's not too far."

"Why don't we take my car? You can drive." She handed me a set of keys, then slipped on some low heels.

"Really? You want me to drive?"

"Sure." She picked up a bottle of wine.

"Oh, I should've told you, I bought flowers for your boss."

"Oh, you didn't have to do that! But thank you, Diane will

appreciate it. I'll still bring the wine because I told her I would."
She winked at me, and we headed out.

When we got out to the street, Brooke waited by her car
while I grabbed the flowers from my truck. Brooke's car was neat
as a pin and smelled like fresh leather. I pulled on my seatbelt
and ran my hands over the steering wheel.

"Very nice," I said. "I'd love to have leather seats someday."

Brooke pulled on her seatbelt. She tossed her hair over her
shoulder and opened her window a little. I opened mine,
inhaling the fresh spring air, and the metallic scent of rain.

"Smells like rain," I said, pulling onto the street.

"Yes, it's supposed to rain later."

"Where are we going, by the way?"

"Greenbriar Street. It's on the other side of town."

"Never heard of it."

The car was a really smooth ride. We drove through downtown and headed across town down a long country road. The
trees on this road grew denser, and the houses were more
spread out.

"Take a right onto this road, this is Greenbriar," she said.

I turned on my signal and took a right into a development
with enormous houses—large brick homes with three stories and
white clapboard homes with circular driveways and three-car
garages.

"Nice street," I said.

"Isn't it? I sold that yellow house last year."

Cripes. The commission on that house alone was probably
half my yearly salary...or more.

"Hers is in the cul-de-sac," she said. "The one with the black
mailbox. You can pull into the driveway and park there."

I slowed down, turned into the driveway, and let out a low
whistle.

"I know, it's amazing. Wait until you see the inside."

A large stone house rose up at the end of the driveway, six, seven, eight windows across the front, and a three-car garage. The front of the house had granite steps and a double front door with cast iron hardware.

I grabbed the flowers, and we headed up the driveway, passing other cars. Brooke took my hand again.

"Oh, I said you were an architect," she said in a low voice. "I hope that's okay."

A flush crept up my neck. She couldn't tell anyone I was a maintenance guy who mopped floors.

"Yeah, fine," I said as she rang the doorbell.

"Oh, and I didn't say how we met because I didn't want to make up an elaborate story. We can figure out something on the fly."

"Sure," I said, bracing myself for whatever came next.

NINE

"Hello! Oh, flowers. Thank you!" Diane greeted us as she opened the door.

"Evan Handler." I handed them to her. "We met at the reception."

"Yes, that's right! Evan. So nice to see you again. Pretty dress, Brooke. Come on in."

Brooke's heels clicked on the tile as we followed Diane down a hall lined with photos into an enormous kitchen. Several people were gathered around a large island with a marble top.

"Everyone, Brooke's here."

"Hey, Brooke."

"Oooh, pretty dress."

"She brought wine!"

Brooke set the wine bottle down and greeted everyone.

"This is my boyfriend, Evan."

Boyfriend, I liked the sound of that better than *friend*. I shook hands and nodded, trying to remember their names. I noticed everyone was paired up with someone. Maybe Brooke just hated going to parties and dinners alone. I didn't blame her.

One of the men opened Brooke's wine and poured some

into glasses. I wasn't a big fan of wine, but I accepted a glass of sparkling water.

"Help yourself," Diane said, pointing to two trays of food. "We have falafel-spiced cucumber bites and pancetta crisps with goat cheese. I don't know why we're congregating in the kitchen. Let's bring everything into the living room, shall we, Martha?"

Martha wore a black shirt and black pants, like a uniform. She was standing at the sink preparing salads.

"Sure," Martha said. "Take your drinks in, and I'll be right there."

As we followed Diane to the living room, I peeked into the dining room and saw two more women clad in black, setting napkins on the table and lighting candles.

"Wow, catering?" I whispered to Brooke.

"Mmm-hmm. Believe me, you don't want Diane to cook," she murmured.

The living room had a vaulted ceiling with wood beams. Two plush couches and chairs offered ample seating, and long drapes framed enormous windows. Potted plants decorated one corner, and large works of contemporary art filled the walls.

I took a seat next to Brooke on a couch. Martha followed us in with the trays of appetizers. As everyone chatted, I put my arm across the back of the couch, and Brooke shifted closer to me, resting her hand on my thigh. I grinned—we had to make it look good.

They talked about houses they'd sold—with swimming pools, acreage, and guest houses.

"Enough shop talk!" Diane said, waving her hand. "We're boring Evan."

"No, it's okay," I said. "I don't mind."

"Brooke says you're an architect," she said, crossing her legs. "Commercial or residential?"

"Residential," I blurted, hoping she wasn't about to quiz me on architecture.

"What kind of homes do you design?" she asked.

"Now, now," Brooke said. "You just said we weren't supposed to talk shop."

"Oh, alright," Diane said.

The talk turned to current movies. I lifted my arm from the back of the couch and squeezed Brooke's shoulder. Her cheek lifted in a small smile, and she snuggled deeper against my side. I liked the feel of her body so close to mine.

A short time later, Martha called us into the dining room. I saw one of the guys pull out a chair for his wife, so I did the same for Brooke. Sitting beside her, I looked at a small card on my plate that listed the night's menu—chestnut fennel soup, wilted spinach salad with warm apple cider and bacon dressing. Butternut squash gnocchi with sage brown butter, pork tenderloins with caramelized pears in a pear-brandy cream sauce. Root vegetable purée, and bourbon cheesecake.

I didn't even know what some of this food *was*, but I was an open-minded eater, and I didn't mind trying the food. But one thing really got my attention.

"*Wilted* lettuce?" I murmured to Brooke.

She put her hand over her mouth and smiled. Everyone took their napkin off their plates as Martha and the caterers started handing out the bowls of soup. The soup was brown and didn't look very appetizing, but I picked up my spoon and gave it a try. It wasn't really appealing, but I got a few spoonfuls down. Brooke wasn't much of a fan, either. I was glad when they came around to take the soup bowls away.

"So, how did you and Evan meet?" a woman named Linda asked.

"I showed him a house," Brooke said, smiling at me. "Isn't that right, honey?"

"Yeah. Yes," I said, trying not to squirm in my chair. "She showed me a house."

"What house?" Linda asked.

"The brick one on Lilac Street," Brooke said.

"Oh, I *love* that house. But you didn't buy it?"

"No," I said. "I'm still looking. I need to find just the right thing."

"You'll know when you find it," Linda said. "But how did it happen? Did you ask for her number?"

A flash of panic crossed Brooke's features, but she smiled at me.

"Why don't you tell the story, Evan?"

I waited a few seconds to gather my thoughts while a salad was put in front of me.

"Well, when Brooke opened the door of that house on Lilac Street, I was struck by how beautiful she was."

"Aww!" the women said.

"I followed her around the house, barely paying attention to the rooms. At the end of the tour, when she asked if I had any questions, I didn't know what to say. But I didn't want to be creepy, so I waited and called her the next day, and she said yes." I took her hand, lifted it to my lips, and kissed it. Her mouth opened a little, and her right eyebrow went up a hair.

"Oh, how sweet!" Linda said. "Charles, you're never romantic like that."

Charles looked up at the mention of his name. He was chewing his salad and swallowed.

"Huh?" he asked.

We chuckled. I squeezed Brooke's hand and released it, trying not to smile too hard. I had some of the wilted salad, realizing wilted just meant warm, but I was dismayed to see pieces of hard-boiled eggs on it.

Next, the gnocchi came, and it was the best thing I'd eaten

so far. I tried to pace myself since there was more food coming. Dinner led to dessert, and the talk turned to schools over coffee. They talked about the colleges their children were attending.

"Where did you go to school, Evan?" Diane asked.

My mouth went dry, but Brooke rescued me again.

"He went to Cornell."

"Oooh, Cornell's a great school," Diane said.

We managed to make it through without any more questions, and I was relieved when it was time to go.

Diane walked us to the door.

"It was nice seeing you again, Evan. Brooke, you've found a good one! Don't let him go!"

Brooke laughed, but it was higher and shriller than her usual husky laugh.

When the door was finally shut behind us, I let out a deep breath until we were in the quiet and safety of the car.

"I am *so* sorry," she said. "I didn't think they'd ask you where you went to college. I had to answer with a college that offered a degree in architecture."

"I'm glad you did, I thought I was screwed."

I turned on the engine and turned around in the driveway, then turned back onto the street.

"I know Cornell has that degree because I looked it up," she said.

"I heard you went to grad school."

"Yes, I... wait, how did you know that?"

"Your assistant mentioned it when I was looking at your awards on the wall. You're one of their top sellers."

"Well, yes." She relaxed in her seat and looked out the window.

"Julia said you were in the top five percent of your class."

She turned to face me. "What else did she tell you that day?"

"Your bra size, and that you like to sleep naked."

Brooke gasped, and I laughed. She hit my arm playfully.

"No, don't worry, she didn't say anything like that, but do you?" I asked.

"Do I what?"

"Sleep naked."

Silence stretched out between us, and I felt my cock shifting at the idea of Brooke sleeping naked.

"No, I do *not* sleep naked."

"Too bad," I said. "But seriously, we need to learn a few more things about each other to make this more realistic."

"I know. I told Diane I hadn't been seeing you for very long. I thought we could make things up on the fly, but we'd better learn a few more facts about each other. For the next time."

I flicked on the turn signal. "So, what's your favorite dessert? Pie with caramelized goat cheese?"

She laughed, using the deep and husky laugh that I liked.

"No, I like cookie dough ice cream."

"I like yellow cake with white buttercream frosting," I said.

"That's very specific."

"My mom used to make it for my birthday."

"Used to? Is she still alive?"

"Yes, but she moved to Arizona to live near her sister after my dad died."

"Oh, I'm so sorry."

"He died when I was a freshman in high school. He had a heart attack at work. We were told he died instantly."

I remembered being called over the intercom to the principal's office on a Tuesday afternoon in the fall. I'd never gotten called to the principal in my life, so when my friends looked at me, I shrugged.

Walking down the long hallway to the principal, I looked at the paper leaves decorating the classroom windows. When I got to the office, I was stunned to see my mother, her face pink and her eyes shiny with tears. She burst into loud sobs when she saw me, and pulled me into her arms while my heart hammered.

The principal closed the door, and my mother told me the news. My skin went cold, but my hands went clammy. My stomach dropped to my feet, and my breathing grew harsh.

"Matty," was all I could say to mom.

"I haven't told him yet," Mom said. "I was hoping..."

"I'll go with you," I said immediately.

"That's my brave boy," she said, hugging me.

I wanted to spare Matty, to run away and pretend it hadn't happened, but I followed Mom out to the car on shaky legs, and we headed over to Matty's school.

"I'm so sorry, Evan." Brooke put her hand on my thigh. "That must have been so difficult."

"Yeah, it was. What about your parents? Do they live around here?"

"They live in Connecticut. I drive down to see them once in a while. I have a sister, Megan. She still lives in Connecticut. She's an engineer."

"Wow, two smart kids in the family. They must be proud."

"Mmm-hmm."

I sensed something there, so I changed the subject.

"I like baseball in the summer and football in the winter. You like sports at all?"

"Not really. I played tennis in college."

"Tennis. Huh. I bet that's harder than it looks."

"It really is. Hey, do you want to see the house on Lilac Street? Take a left here."

I took a left and found myself on a street with houses almost as big as Diane's. The car's headlights swept over fences and mailboxes.

"There," Brooke said. "This brick house on the left."

I slowed down, peering at the large brick house with a nice front yard and a two-car garage. A few windows were lit with lamps.

"Awesome, I'm loaded," I said. "How much is this house?"

"It's four ninety-nine."

I sucked in a breath. "Meaning four-hundred and ninety-nine *thousand*? As in half a million dollars?"

"Yes."

"Jesus. My house growing up was brick, but it was a small ranch. What was your house like growing up?"

"It was a colonial. My parents still live there."

We spent the ride back to the hotel exchanging a few more details, so next time we'd be more prepared.

I was sorry when we pulled into the hotel parking lot, since I wanted to spend more time with her. Turning off the engine, I released my seat belt. Brooke released her own seatbelt and put her hand on my thigh. This touch had a different meaning. It was firm and high on my thigh.

"Want to come upstairs?" she asked.

I closed my hand over hers.

"I'm a full-service escort, so yeah, let's go see your bedroom."

TEN

The ride up the elevator in the hotel seemed to take forever. We walked down the long hallway, and Brooke unlocked the door to her suite. A lamp was lit in the living room.

She kicked her shoes off. I did the same, following her to the closed door I'd seen before. Opening the door, she flicked on the light switch. The enormous bed had several pillows arranged by the padded headboard.

"Is this bed as comfy as it looks?" I asked.

"It's incredible. The mattress is so comfortable, and the sheets are to die for."

I sat at the end of the bed and bounced a little.

"Nice."

Brooke moved back to the light switch and turned it off.

"Hey," I said. "Why'd you do that?"

"A woman likes to have *some* mystery."

"But now I can barely see you."

The light from the living room was dim, but my eyes had adjusted a little, and I could see she was unbuttoning her dress. She pushed it down over her hips and slipped it off, standing before me in her bra and panties.

Putting her hand on my shoulder, she leaned over and pressed a soft kiss on my lips. Her skin was velvety soft, and my cock started growing. I spent time kissing and stroking her skin, wondering how I'd gotten so damn lucky.

She suddenly pulled away from me and walked to the far side of the bed, pulling down the comforter and the sheet. I stood and reached for my zipper, but she came back and pushed my hands away, unzipping me herself.

Her hand slid into my pants, and she felt my rigid cock bulging through my underwear. I let out a long sigh as she stroked me through the fabric.

"Tell me what you like, Brooke."

"I like being kissed on my neck."

I pushed her hair back over her shoulder and kissed her neck. She sighed and pulled me closer. Kissing her neck and shoulder, I inhaled the powdery scent of her skin. She tugged at the waistband of my underwear, then slipped her hand inside.

"Oh, fuck," I said.

She stroked me with her small, soft fingers, and my eyes slid shut. I desperately wanted to be inside her, but I didn't want to rush. Her stroking grew faster and more insistent. She released me and pushed my pants down. I stepped out of them and unbuttoned my shirt, tossing it aside.

Brooke slipped off her bra and underwear, then climbed into bed. I finished stripping and climbed in beside her, wishing I could see more of her curvy, sexy body.

We kissed for several minutes, touching and sighing. I reached down and grabbed her ass, squeezing it, loving the feel of her softness in my hands. I was enjoying the kissing when she sat up and straddled me.

"You know what else I like?" she asked.

She leaned over and kissed my neck, working her way down

my chest. I closed my eyes and surrendered to the sensation of her mouth on my skin. She moved lower and lower until she took me into her mouth. I cursed again, digging my fingers into the sheets. I hadn't gotten a blow job a long time, and I was desperate not to come too soon. She pulled me in deeper, swiping her tongue over the head, getting it nice and wet, using her hands to stroke my shaft.

"Damn, you're good at this," I said.

"Do you like how I'm doing this?" she asked.

"Yes. Oh, yes."

She put her mouth back on me, and the familiar tingling was building up in my balls. I concentrated on holding back, but she was just so damn sexy, working me so good, and her mouth was so hot and wet.

I let out a long, shaky moan, wondering if I should warn her about my imminent explosion. I don't know how long she sucked me, teasing me to the edge, then slowing down. My legs grew stiff, and I gasped, bucking my hips. She took me in nice and deep, not letting up with her sucking and stroking.

"Wait!" I said.

"It's okay," she said. "Let me taste you."

I put my hand on her head and gave in to the suction of her lips, and then came with a shout, my upper body lifting off the bed. She took all of it, licking and sucking until I finished. She released me, and lay beside me, panting.

"That was incredible," I said. "I would've done that for free."

She laughed, and I wrapped my arms around her, stroking her back.

"I love how you taste," she said.

"Can I find out how you taste?" I asked.

She nodded, and I slid down her body, settling between her legs. There was nothing I liked more than going down on a woman—except maybe going down on a woman for the first time, learning what she liked, and listening to her moans.

I brushed my fingers over her pussy, and her scent filled my nostrils. Even her hair down here was soft and fragrant. Kissing her upper thighs, I enjoyed her harsh intake of breath. And when I slid my tongue into her folds, I found delicious, musky wetness. When I found her clit, I licked it with firm, steady pressure. She moaned and grabbed a handful of my hair. I kept going, thoroughly enjoying the wetness and her sexy moans.

I paused to open her thighs, spreading her wider for me. She released my head, grabbing the pillow and writhing on the mattress. I took my time, loving the taste and feel of her. When I slipped a finger inside her, she practically levitated. Her wetness doubled, which I took as a good sign. I fucked her with my finger, teasing her clit with my mouth, listening to her cues.

"Oh!" she cried out. "Oh..."

Fuck, she was sexy. I liked working her into a frenzy of moans. Her thighs started shaking, and I curled my finger inside her.

"Ahhh! Oh, Evan."

I sped up, encouraged by her moans, and when I applied more pressure to her clit, she finally exploded, crying out and bucking against my face. I kept licking her until I was satisfied that she was finished.

She was still breathing heavy when I came back up to lie beside her. Putting my arm around her, I pulled her against me. Her heart pounded a steady rhythm against my chest. I listened to the sound of her breathing and stroked her hair.

A few minutes later, she moved and pulled the covers up over us. I closed my eyes and started to doze. I hated to fall asleep so quickly, but I became a zombie once I came.

"Should go," I mumbled.

"Hmm?"

"I should go before I get too sleepy."

"You don't have to go," she said.

"I'd love to stay, but I get up pretty early, and I don't have any of my stuff here."

"I understand."

Her warm body was nestled against me just right. I stroked her hair and listened to her soft breathing. I'd almost forgotten the closeness of holding a woman in bed. She was so sexy and fun, and I wanted to know everything about her.

"Tell me something else. About your childhood, or where you went to school," I said.

"Oh, I had a pretty standard childhood. I had some good friends at school and in the neighborhood. Except for one boy who used to pull my ponytail."

I chuckled.

"I got my revenge, though. One day, I was playing kickball at recess with my friends. The bully came over and grabbed the ball. I marched right over to him, grabbed it back, and shoved him hard. He pushed me. I pushed him back, and he fell on his ass. He called me every swear word in the book, but he stopped pushing me around."

I grinned. "Atta girl."

"What about you? Tell me something about your childhood."

I tried to push away the bad memories and focused on the good.

"I liked to build treehouses with my brother. He's six years younger, and most of the time I saw him as a pesky little brother. We didn't like the same things and we had different friends. But when we went into the backyard and worked on our treehouse, we had fun. We spent hours in there, playing with baseball cards and reading comic books."

"Are you two still close?"

"Yeah. He's graduating from college soon. He's going to stay there and work for the summer, but I was hoping to be in a house by the time he comes home. He usually spends the summer on the couch in our apartment. It's not ideal, but he's a good sport about it. I really need a place for us to live, and I want to buy a house."

"I can help you with that."

"The kinda houses I'm looking at won't be on Lilac street. A small two- or three-bedroom ranch would do it. A fixer-upper, so it costs less. It's not exactly the kind of house you usually sell."

"No, but I know the area really well. I know the neighborhoods and other agents who sell smaller homes. I can definitely help you."

I hugged her. "I get sex *and* real estate help. I'm glad we met."

"I don't want you to leave," she said quietly.

"I know. I'll pack my stuff and bring it over tomorrow night. How's that sound?"

"Sounds like I'm getting my money's worth."

She put her hand on my cheek and softly kissed me. I finally tore myself away and got dressed. She pulled on a robe from the bathroom and walked me to the door.

"Goodnight," I said, stroking her cheek with my thumb.

"Goodnight, Evan."

And then she closed the door behind me.

ELEVEN

The next day seemed to drag. I usually didn't mind my job, but it seemed like the clock was moving backward. I kept getting calls to drop what I was doing to go fix some emergency, which meant I had to go back and finish some incomplete jobs.

It felt like an eternity had gone by, but it was only lunchtime. I ate in the lunchroom with Frank and the other guys. They talked about their wives and kids. Brooke was on my mind, but I didn't dare bring her up.

My radio beeped when I was packing up my lunch bag.

"Evan? It's Carly. Do you have a minute?"

I picked up my radio. "Sure, what do you need?"

"One of the residents said he's having trouble with his circuit breaker."

"Be right there."

I walked out to Carly's desk. She was holding a resident work order and frowning.

"You don't look too happy," I said.

"I was having a good day until *he* called."

"Who?"

"Mr. Jacobs," she said, lowering her voice. "The jerk with the package yesterday."

"Great."

"He thinks his circuit breaker blew a fuse or something. Half his kitchen and living room lights don't turn on." She handed me the work order.

"Okay, I'm headed up there now."

"Good luck."

I headed up to the sixth floor and knocked on his door. He flung it open.

"Oh, it's you," he said, scowling.

"Evan," I said, pointing to my name tag.

"Well, come in."

I walked in, scanning his condo. It was always surprising to see the different ways the residents furnished their homes. Brad's condo was filled with high-end leather chairs and glass tables. There were two laptops and a printer on the kitchen table. It looked cold and sterile, especially compared to the coziness of Brooke's place.

"It's about time you got here," he said. "I called fifteen minutes ago. There's something wrong with the circuit breaker. I opened the panel, but I couldn't figure out the problem."

What an ass. I walked over to the electrical panel to take a look.

"Have you touched any of these?" I asked, knowing the answer.

"Well, yes. I just touched this one. And this one, too."

I walked over to the kitchen light switch and turned it on—nothing. I turned on a second light, and then a third—nothing. I had to go back downstairs to get some gear.

"I'll be back in a few minutes," I said. "I need to get some supplies."

"Make it fast, please. I have a meeting here in twenty minutes! I have a slide show to present."

"Mr. Jacobs, you can book one of the conference rooms downstairs for your meeting. They're pretty quiet this time of day, I'm sure one's available."

"If I wanted to book a conference room, I would have. I wanted to have it here. More homey."

I glanced at the bare windows and chrome and glass surfaces—homey... sure.

"I'll be right back," I assured him.

I came back with some tools. I was pretty good at fixing electrical problems. Brad hovered around me as I worked, but I quickly finished and packed up my tools.

"Just try not to overload the circuits," I said.

"This building is only three years old. There shouldn't be anything wrong with the electrical panel."

I closed my toolbox and hoisted it up. "You can have problems if you run too many things at once to just a few plugs. You have two computers here, a printer, and I see a blender on the counter. And your dryer is on. The washer and dryer are on the same circuit as the kitchen."

"I was making a smoothie."

I had to bite the inside of my cheek to keep from laughing.

"Well, try to keep the multitasking to a minimum."

Later that afternoon, I stopped by Carly's desk and told her about Brad.

"*I was making a smoothie?* He really said that?" she asked, her face pink from laughter.

"Yeah. What does he do, anyway? I've seen him in a suit. Doesn't he go to an office?"

"He does, but he also works from home some days."

"Always an adventure. Catch you later, Carly."

I had a few more things to clean up, then it was time to go home.

* * *

LIAM STOOD in the doorway to my room as I packed a bag. His arms were crossed, and he was frowning.

"So, you're really doing this whole gigolo thing?"

"Yup." I tossed my deodorant in my bag. "It's just for a couple of weeks. We'll be out late some nights, and you know I get up early. She gets up pretty early, too. What's the big deal? Throw a party! Have the guys over."

"Hmph," he said. "Have you told Matty about this arrangement?"

I shot him a look. "No, and he doesn't need to know about it, either."

"Okay, okay."

"What's the big deal? You'll get more privacy for a couple of weeks. Bring a girl home. Swing from the chandelier."

"That seems to be your line of expertise."

I zipped my bag shut. "We haven't swung from the chandeliers yet."

"But you *have* slept with her, right? Come on, give me some details!"

"We might have, but I'm not telling you anything else, you perv."

"Is she a freak? She probably acts all demure, selling those big houses. But she has a dungeon and whips you, right?"

"No, she doesn't have a dungeon or whips. Get a grip."

I opened my closet and took out my few nice clothes. I'd gotten my jacket and nice pants dry cleaned, and they were wrapped in plastic bags. I headed for the door. Liam followed, looking sullen.

"You can call me any time," I said. "The two weeks will be over, and I'll be back here getting in your way."

"Yeah, sure. Listen, are you *sure* she doesn't have a rich friend who also needs a gigolo? I'm up for the challenge."

"Goodbye, Liam."

I opened the door and stepped into the hallway. Liam flipped me off, then shut and locked the door. I laughed and headed to the hotel.

* * *

BROOKE HAD JUST GOTTEN BACK to the room when I arrived. I put my bag in the bedroom and hung my clothes in the closet.

"Have you had dinner yet?" she asked. "I'm starving."

"No. I was hoping you'd like to go out tonight."

"Why don't we go to the restaurant downstairs? I've eaten there a few times."

I hesitated. I didn't know what the prices were like in the restaurant, but I was betting it was pretty expensive. I had cash on me; I just hoped it was enough.

"Sure," I said. "I should change, though."

I'd worn my nicer dark jeans and a polo shirt in an effort to look somewhat nice. Brooke was impeccably dressed in a skirt, a silky looking blouse, and heels.

"No, you're fine," she said. "You look nice."

"But I'm wearing jeans."

"People walk into the restaurant all the time wearing jeans."

"Okay, then. I just need to hit the bathroom first."

Once I closed the bathroom door, I pulled out my wallet and counted my cash. I had sixty-three dollars. More than enough for dinner and beers at Cooper's, but it probably wouldn't get us very far in the hotel restaurant. I had a credit card, but I was trying not to use it much while I saved for a house.

Brooke chatted about work on the way downstairs. Her phone rang in her purse as we were about to enter the restaurant. She took out her phone and looked at the display.

"I need to get this. I'm sorry, Evan. Can you get us a table? I'll be right there."

"Sure," I said. I walked up to the hostess stand, and the woman standing there looked me up and down.

"Can I help you?" she asked.

"I'd like a table for two, please."

She looked down at her paper and frowned. "It'll be about thirty minutes for a table. Can I get your name?"

The restaurant looked half-empty, but I gave my name and sat in the small waiting area. A few minutes later, Brooke came in and found me.

"All done. How long is the wait?"

"Miss Sinclair?" the hostess asked.

Brooke turned and looked at her. "Yes?"

"I didn't know the table was for you. Come right this way, and I'll get you seated."

"Thank you," Brooke said.

I tried to glare at the hostess when we sat down, but she didn't look at me. She dropped off our menus and said our waitress would be right over.

"Hmm, she told me it would be a thirty-minute wait, but once you showed up, we got right in."

"Really? I have no idea why."

Opening the menu, I tried to put it out of my mind. I looked at the menu, and my heart stopped for a second. These prices were insane! Thirty-nine dollars for a small piece of steak? Eight dollars for a side of potatoes. The credit card was gonna get a good workout tonight.

"What's good here?" I asked.

"Everything I've tried so far is good. The steak is very good."

The waitress came over and took our drink orders. I ordered a beer. Brooke ordered a glass of white wine and put her menu down.

"I don't think a restaurant like this is what you're used to."

"Nope, but I'm not fussy. I'll eat nearly anything, except calamari. I draw the line there."

Brooke laughed. "Why don't we go somewhere else?"

"We just ordered drinks. Besides, I'm starvin', and you said you're hungry, too."

"We'll order an appetizer. The chicken fajita flatbread is really good. Then you can take me to your favorite place."

"The flatbread sounds like a great plan, but I'm not sure my favorite place suits you, either. It's a run-down sports bar, filled with guys like me who swear, burp, and yell at games on the TV."

"It sounds like fun! That's what we'll do, then." She closed her menu and smiled, looking pleased with herself.

"Okay. But you'll have to change outta that skirt and heels. Do you have any jeans?"

"Yes, I do."

I raised an eyebrow.

"I do have jeans, I promise."

"And wear shoes that don't cost a fortune. There are peanut shells on the floor sometimes." I drummed my fingers on the table. "You sure you want to go there?"

"Yes," she said firmly.

"Okay, then. Cooper's Tavern, here we come."

TWELVE

After we finished our drink and appetizers, I paid, and we left. Brooke tried to pay the bill, but I grabbed it. I put my credit card down so I'd have enough cash for the bar.

When Brooke went upstairs to change, I sat in the lobby and texted Liam, letting him know we were on our way over. He called me immediately.

"Are you *nuts*? Don't bring her here!"

"Why? Is everyone drunker than usual?" It was loud in the background, but I knew there wasn't a game on tonight.

"No, but you know how rowdy they get sometimes. It's one of those nights already. We ate, and now we're playing darts. I'm half in the bag, myself." He let out a short burp in my ear.

"I suggested it might not be a great idea, but she insisted. You think you could tell the guys to settle down just a bit tonight?"

Liam laughed so long and hard, I pulled the phone away, then he hung up. A few seconds later, he texted me a photo of him and Drew holding beer bottles and smiling. I didn't hear Brooke approaching and jumped a little when she said my name.

She wore a red V-neck shirt with three-quarter length sleeves, dark jeans that hugged every curve, and brown leather boots.

"You look amazing," I said.

She really did, but she was still wearing nice jewelry and carrying her brown leather purse that probably cost more than my truck. Even in more casual clothes, it was clear this woman had expensive taste.

"Thank you, Evan."

I stood, and she approached, carrying her floral scent. She stood on her toes and placed a small kiss on my lips that warmed my chest.

"Brace yourself," I said as she took my hand.

* * *

COOPER'S WAS a little subdued when we walked in. My friends were sitting at their usual tables, with beer bottles in front of them.

"Hey, there he is!"

"He's slumming it!"

"Hey, Evan, you got that twenty bucks you owe me?"

"Very funny," I said. "Everyone, this is Brooke. Brooke, this is Max, Drew, Travis, and Liam. Liam's my roommate."

"Hi," Brooke said. "It smells so good in here."

"We just ordered from Jenna a couple minutes ago," Liam said. "You two hungry?"

The flatbread appetizer at the hotel was good, but it was tiny and had barely tamped down my hunger.

"Yeah," I said.

"Come sit here," Liam said, patting the seat beside him.

I shot him a look and took the seat next to him instead, leaving the seat across from me open. Brooke sat down, but that left her open to being ogled face-to-face by Liam. He had a goofy smile on his face, and I could tell he was buzzed.

"Yo, Jenna!" Liam yelled, making Brooke jump.

"Yeah, yeah," Jenna said. "Be right over."

"Do they have menus?" Brooke asked.

"Well, there's a menu written in chalk over the bar, but you should just order the burger and fries basket. It's wicked good here."

"Okay, I'll do that."

Jenna came over, her blonde ponytail looking a little bedraggled today.

"What do you jerks—I mean, what do you fine gentlemen need?" she asked, taking her pen from behind her ear. She looked Brooke up and down. "You're new here."

"I'm Brooke Sinclair. How are you?"

Jenna's mouth dropped open, and she looked at me, then back at Brooke.

"Good. I'm Jenna. You guys ordering baskets?"

"Yes," I said.

"How do you want yours cooked, honey?" she asked Brooke.

"Medium. And I'll have a beer. What do you have?"

I suggested my favorite local craft beer, and Jenna left to put in our order.

"So, what do you do for work, Brooke?" Liam asked, acting dumb.

"I'm an agent with Turner Real Estate. Here's my card." She pulled out a card and handed it to him.

"Really?" Liam took the card. "You know Evan's looking for a house."

"Yes, he told me. I'm going to help him."

"Oh, yeah?" he asked. "So, what do you like to do for fun?"

"Hey, come on," I said. "Don't grill her. She just got here!"

"It's fine, Evan. Really."

Jenna came back with our beer bottles. "Here ya go. Your burgers will be out in a few."

"Thanks," we said.

Brooke took a sip of her beer. "This is good!"

"Glad you like it," I said. "Hey, do you ever play darts?"

Some of the guys had gotten up to play, arguing over who was first.

"I played some back in college," she said. "I'm not very good."

"I beat Liam most of the time."

"Hey! You do not. I trounce his ass most of the time."

"After we eat, I'll kick your ass in front of everyone," I said.

"Looking forward to it. I'm gonna join the guys."

He got up and left us alone at the tables to join the other guys, who had started playing. A group of guys in the back burst out in raucous laughter. Behind the bar, Jenna turned up the music, classic rock blaring out of the speakers.

"Not a great place to talk," I said.

"It's okay. This is a lot more fun than the Carlisle."

The guys broke out in laughter after one of them missed the dartboard completely, but my eyes were drawn to Brooke. Even though she was still overdressed for the place, she looked good here. She looked at home.

We started talking about everything and nothing—what kind of food we liked and didn't like, pets we had growing up, what we wanted to be when we were kids.

Jenna brought over our baskets of food, extra napkins, and ketchup.

"Here ya go. Just holler if you need anything else."

We tucked in. I watched with interest as Brooke picked up her burger in her small hands, trying to get a grip on it. When she managed a bite, she moaned.

"Oh, you're right, this is so good."

"Told ya. If you can stand the ambiance, this place has the best burgers and fries."

"It's good we're talking like this. Getting to know each other will help the next time we're questioned on anything."

Ouch. And here I was getting to know her because I was interested in her. But she was right, this was a business transaction, after all. I had to play the part, then I could get my money.

After we finished eating, I looked over at the guys. "Wanna play?"

She wiped her mouth with a napkin. "Aren't they still playing?"

"No, they just finished. Wanna give it a try?"

"Sure."

We got up and went over to the guys.

"Hey, Brooke wants a turn."

"Here you go," Drew said, handing over some darts.

"Okay, where do I stand?" she asked.

I pointed to a spot on the wooden floor, worn down by years and thousands of shoes.

"Right here."

She picked up the first dart, aimed, and threw.

"Not bad," I said. "Try again."

She tossed another, and it landed close to the center.

"Oooh!" Drew said. "Liam, she's better than you!"

"Shut up!" Liam said.

Brooke laughed. The next time, her throw was off, and the dart hit the wall and bounced onto the floor. Drew scurried over to get the darts for her.

"Here, try again," he said.

"You throw like a girl," Travis said.

"I *am* a girl," Brooke said, pushing her hair out of her face.

"Here, let me show you." Travis came forward with a dart. "Stand like this."

He put his hand on Brooke's hip and turned her a little. "Now, try holding it like this."

He put his hand on hers, and jealousy clawed at my insides. Travis was a lady-killer, always flirting and touching women, and they usually fell for it.

"Don't listen to him," I said. "There are different ways to stand and throw. Just do what's comfortable for you."

"Chill out, Handler," Travis said. "Just trying to help."

She threw the three darts again and didn't do half bad. Drew handed me some darts, and I tossed a few.

"You're good," Brooke said.

Most of the guys sat back at the tables. Travis lingered nearby, much to my annoyance. Brooke and I took turns playing. Her cheeks grew pink as she laughed and threw darts.

"Oh, damn!" she said. "That was an awful throw."

I put my arm around her and pulled her in for a kiss. Her eyes closed as she pressed her lips to mine.

"Hmph," Travis said, wandering off.

"Hey, get a room!" Drew yelled.

Brooke blushed. I put a possessive hand on her hip.

"Wanna get out of here?"

She looked up at me through her dark lashes. Damn, her eyes were such a pretty shade of blue.

"Yes," she said.

Good. I wanted to get her out of those jeans and spend more time exploring her body.

"We're gonna take off," I told the guys, pulling out my wallet to pay for our food and drinks. I knew exactly how much it was and included a healthy tip for Jenna. I tossed the bills on the table.

"Aw, come on."

"You just got here!"

"Where's my twenty bucks?"

"Have another beer."

"Nah, I'll see you guys later," I said.

Brooke picked up her bag. "It was nice to meet you all."

"See ya!"

"Bye."

"Don't do anything I would," Travis said, wiggling his brows.

I took Brooke's hand, and we headed out. Once we got back to my truck, Brooke turned in her seat to look at me.

"I don't think you liked it when Travis touched me."

I started the engine. "I'm not usually the jealous type, but no, I didn't like it."

"Well, you have nothing to worry about. Take me back to the room, and I'll prove it."

My cock was growing in my jeans. I pulled out of the parking lot and tried not to speed.

THIRTEEN

Back in the suite, I tossed my keys and wallet on the table while Brooke sat down and pulled off her boots.

"Oh, I have an extra key for you," she said. "And I added you as a guest at the desk."

She walked over to the counter and picked up a key and handed it to me.

"It's funny that they still use old keys. Thanks."

I put the key aside and kicked off my shoes. Brooke grabbed my hand, led me to the bedroom. She immediately reached for my jeans and started unbuttoning them.

"Now," she said. "About Travis. He's the flirty type, always touching. Standing too close." She unzipped my jeans, revealing the bulge in my underwear. "I've been with guys like that. But I like you. I chose you."

I slid my hands into her hair and kissed her, pushing her back until we reached the edge of the bed. I stopped and tugged off my clothes.

Brooke pulled off her shirt, and I helped to remove her jeans, sliding them down over her curvy hips and calves. Pulling her against me, I kissed her again, my cock pressing against her through the fabric of my underwear. I reached behind her and unfastened her bra, tossing it aside.

Grabbing her by the waist, I tossed her on the bed, and she laughed. I climbed onto the bed and hovered above her, just taking her in—her soft breasts, the gold chain at her neck, and the cute pair of hip-hugging underwear just begging to be pulled off.

"Can I take these off?" I asked her.

"Yes."

I peeled them off and tossed them aside, and then laid beside her. We kissed again, more urgently this time, her tongue pressing against mine. I grabbed her thigh and lifted it over my hip. Her skin was so warm with her breasts pressing against my chest.

My cock was like iron, jabbing against her. We spent a long time kissing and stroking each other. I wanted to be inside her, but I was thoroughly enjoying the foreplay.

I pushed her onto her back and slid my hand down to her pussy.

"I've been thinking about getting you naked all day," I said.

"Ohhh."

Her nails dug into my arm, and she squirmed under my touch. She was damp, but I wanted her soaking wet. I kissed her neck, then sucked on her earlobe.

"You're so damned sexy. Every guy in Cooper's was checking you out, but I liked knowing you're mine."

Kissing her breast, I drew her nipple into my mouth until it pebbled. Warm fluid rushed over my fingers, and I rubbed her clit until her breathing grew ragged.

"Evan! Oh!"

"That's good. So damn good. Are you getting close? Am I doing it right?"

"Yes!"

Her thighs clamped together, and she came, crying out and digging her fingernails into my arm. She bucked and moved against my hand, so sexy, powerful, and beautiful. I kept rubbing until she moved my hand away.

"Should I get a condom?" I asked.

"Yes."

I scurried off the bed, my cock bobbing comically in front of me, and dug into my pocket until I came up with a strip of three condoms—a hopeful amount.

Tearing one off, I opened it and rolled it on. Climbing back on the bed, I hovered over her again, rubbing my cock against her. She reached down, holding my shaft, and guided me inside, and I slowly sank into her heat.

She put her hands on my cheeks and pulled me down for a kiss. I waited a few seconds before starting to move. She felt incredible, and hiked her legs up around my hips.

"Oh, God," she said.

I reached under her thigh, hiking it up around my waist. Our movements were slow at first, then after several minutes, grew more frantic. I moaned and swore, knowing I wasn't going to last.

"You feel so. Damn. Good," I said.

I slowed down, wanting to last, but that familiar tingle started in my balls. I slid forward, grinding hard against her clit, wanting her to come, and she tightened around me.

Her legs squeezed me, and her heels dug into my thighs. I didn't want it to end, but she cried out, coming, squeezing me hard, and I quickly followed, grinding hard against her and moaning.

"Damn," I said when we finished. "Damn."

A few minutes later, I slipped off her and went to the bathroom to ditch the condom. When I got back, she was lying on her side, smiling.

"Hope you got your money's worth," I said.

"You should charge extra for that technique of yours."

I climbed back into bed and kissed her, then settled on the pillow facing her.

"So, why do you want to buy a house so badly?" she asked.

"I'm getting sick of apartment living. I want a yard where I can grill out with my friends, play football. Hell, I want to mow the lawn. Or make Matty do it."

"So, what's your brother getting his degree in?"

"Sports medicine."

"That sounds interesting."

"Yeah, he's done really well. He even hit the dean's list a few times. I never thought he'd even go to college, let alone finish."

"Why not?" she asked.

"Matty had a drug problem when he got out of high school. He took a year off to work and think about going to college. He met some other kids at work who gave him pot, then he moved onto harder drugs."

"That must have been hard."

"Yup. My mom was devastated. We finally talked him into going to rehab. Well, forced him into it, really."

"Did it work?" she asked.

"We got a call one day that he'd left. Just up and left. My mom was hysterical. We drove around everywhere he used to hang out. Finally, he showed back up at rehab about twelve hours later."

I remembered the heart-pounding panic as I climbed into the car and drove Mom around. She had her purse on her lap and kept twisting her hands around the handle. Her face got paler and paler the more places we stopped.

When I pulled up to one of Matty's druggie friends at two in the morning, my mom begged me not to go in.

"But what if he's in there, Ma?"

She started to cry. I got out of the car and went up the sidewalk to the front door. I pounded on it, and eventually a woman with dark hair opened the door.

"What the hell?" she asked.

I pushed my way inside. "Is Ray here? Where is he?"

"Who the hell are you? Get out of my house! RAYYYYY!"

"What the fuck, Ma?"

Ray came out of his room, rubbing his eyes and scowling. He stopped when he saw me.

"Where. Is. Matty?" I stalked over and shoved him against the wall so hard, the pictures rattled. "Where is he?"

"Dunno. I haven't seen him since he went to rehab!"

"I'm calling the cops," his mom said, picking up her phone.

I walked past both of them and looked in the bedrooms and bathroom for Matty. When I came out, they were just staring at me, open-mouthed.

"Get the fuck out of my house!" Ray yelled.

"Stay the hell away from my brother!" I said, jabbing his chest with my finger. "You got me? Stay away from him!"

"Alright, man! Jesus!"

I stalked out of the house, slamming the door. Mom was silent in the car. Finally, we headed home to eat and get some rest. I had just pulled into the driveway when the phone rang. The rehab center called, saying he came back.

My mom sobbed in relief. I put my head on the steering wheel and closed my eyes, then I went into the house and slept for nine hours straight in my old bedroom. After Mom and I got up and ate, we went back to rehab to see Matty and talk to the doctors.

Matty had dark circles under his eyes. He said he just couldn't stand being cooped up in there anymore and went out to walk around and get something to eat. He said he didn't use any drugs, but I didn't believe him.

"He went back and finished, and when he got out, he applied at colleges and worked until the acceptances started rolling in. He's smart as hell. I knew he'd do okay once he got clean."

"It'll be nice for you two to have a house," she said. "I can understand that."

"I know he won't live with me forever. But I figured it would be nice for me to have a home when I meet someone and get married someday."

Silence. Several seconds ticked by before I realized what I'd said.

"I mean, *if* I get married someday."

"Sure," she said.

Fuck. For some reason, I felt bad.

"Are you hungry?" she asked. "I have some ice cream in the freezer."

"Sure," I said. "Let me guess. Cookie dough?"

"Yup. Do you like it?"

"Yeah, I'll have some."

She got up and put on her robe. She rustled around in the kitchen, scooping ice cream into bowls. I looked down at the messy sheets. I was having fun with Brooke, but this was just for a couple of weeks. I'd get paid and turn in my key, and I'd be out of her life.

"Okay, here we go, cookie dough ice cream."

I sat up, and she gave me a bowl. It was a cozy scene, me and my nakedness, covered only by a sheet. And Brooke with her messy hair and bathrobe.

It was the kind of thing I'd do with a girlfriend...or a wife.

Any guy would love to be in my position—having sex for a paycheck. I just didn't count on just how smart and sexy this woman would turn out to be, or how much I would like her.

I was starting to see just how complicated this could get.

FOURTEEN

A few days later, I went to the suit shop after work to order a tuxedo and picked up my other clothes. I couldn't believe I was getting fitted for a tux, but we were going to a big fundraiser, and it was formal.

"Why can't I just rent a tux?" I'd asked her last night.

"Every man needs a tuxedo," she said. "Besides, you'll be wearing it twice. Once for the fundraiser, and for the awards dinner."

"Still, I could rent one twice."

"But a fitted tuxedo will look so much better," she insisted.

I stopped arguing since it wasn't worthwhile.

"What are you wearing?" I asked.

"I ordered a dress online and brought it to my seamstress for alterations."

"You have a seamstress?"

"She's not my *personal* seamstress. I go to her shop in town."

The men at the shop were more accommodating now that they knew I had money to spend. They certainly wouldn't have given me a second look otherwise.

"What color tie would you like?" the salesman asked me.

"Black," I said.

Brooke had told me to get a simple black bowtie. I didn't even know how to tie a bowtie.

"Could you show me how to tie this? I've never worn one before."

"Certainly. Come over to the mirror and I'll show you."

He put one on, showing me what to do. Then I put it on. It took me a few tries to make it look right.

"Excellent," he said. "Try it a few more times before the big night, and you'll do fine."

I paid for the tux and arranged to pick it up another day. Then I texted Liam to see if he was free, but he didn't answer. My nerves were jittery, and I found myself taking out my phone and calling Julia.

"Evan," she said. "How can I help you? Did you get the tuxedo?"

"Yeah, I paid for one, and they have to make some alterations. But I have a problem, and I was wondering if you could help me out."

* * *

AN HOUR LATER, I was sitting in a small conference room at Turner Real Estate with Julia. She had laid out a formal place setting on the table with all the utensils, glasses, and plates. I had no idea where she got everything, but I didn't question it. She had even arranged a red cloth napkin in a rose shape.

"Water glass. White wine glass. Red wine glass. Champagne glass."

"Jesus, *four* glasses?" I asked.

"I'm not sure how many glasses they'll use, so I'm showing you four. On the left—salad fork, fish fork, dinner fork."

"Fish fork?" I grinned. "You need a special fork to eat fish?"

"If there's a fish course. But you might only have two forks, the salad, and the dinner fork."

She went over the knives and spoons, then quizzed me on everything.

"Now," she said. "What's the first thing you do?"

I looked at the utensils, trying to remember everything.

"I pick up the salad fork—"

"No, you need to spread the napkin on your lap."

I picked it up and pulled it open, then placed it on my lap.

"Don't flop it around."

"I wasn't *flopping* it."

She took it from me and expertly rolled it back into a rose shape and placed it back on the plate.

"Try again."

I tried again, then she walked me through a meal, making sure I touched each utensil. She even went over what to do after the meal, including the placement of utensils, and putting my napkin down.

"I think you'll be proficient now," she said.

"Thanks, Julia."

"And don't forget to pull out Brooke's chair every time she goes to sit down. And try not to curse. And be polite."

"I know."

She gave me a lopsided smile. "You'll do fine. Good luck, Evan."

* * *

THE NIGHT of the fundraiser quickly approached. I'd picked up my tuxedo and practiced tying my bow tie until it came out perfectly.

I was thoroughly servicing Brooke in bed every night. She was good at communicating what she did and didn't like, and she was so responsive to my touches. I kissed her goodbye in the morning, wearing my uniform as she ate breakfast in her robe. At the end of each day, she greeted me with a kiss.

We took turns cooking dinner in the small kitchen and going out to eat. Brooke had fronted me more cash to pay for our dinners out.

"You can take it out of my final pay," I told her.

"Not necessary," she said, as if handing over six hundred dollars in cash was no big deal.

The night of the fundraiser, I got dressed, carefully tying the perfect bow in my tie. Brooke was in the shower, and Julia had come over to help.

"Stay in the living room while we get ready," Julia said. "Or better yet, go wait downstairs at the bar. Don't have more than one drink, though."

"Why do I have to wait down there? I can just stay in the living room while you help her in the bedroom."

"She'll want to make an entrance," Julia said. "Let her have that. Downstairs and at the event. Remember, you're supposed to be the charming but supportive boyfriend who fades into the woodwork."

"Gee, thanks."

"It's nothing personal, Evan. It'll make her feel special. Now go wait downstairs."

"Fine."

Grabbing my wallet, I went down to the lobby. I checked my appearance in the mirror—tie, straight. Hair...mostly straight. Shoes, nice and shiny. I had to go to another store to pick out new black shoes and socks.

I paced a little over the plush carpet in the lobby, then I went into the large restaurant bar. I thought about going to the small bar in the back to see if Charlie was there, but from here, I could see her as she walked through the lobby. Part of the restaurant's walls were glass, and I watched people walk in and out of the hotel.

The restaurant was pretty quiet, with only a few people sitting at tables eating. A man sat nursing a tall glass of beer at the other end of the bar as I slid onto a stool.

"Nice tux," the bartender said. "Heading to a party?"

"A fundraiser," I said.

"Cool. I'm Amanda. What can I get you?"

I ordered a soda, which I drank slowly. I kept checking my watch. Why did it take women so damn long to get ready?

"Waiting for someone?" Amanda asked.

"Yeah, my girlfriend is getting ready."

Girlfriend. I was surprised at how easily the word rolled off my tongue.

"Well, she wants to look good."

"She'd look good in a potato sack," I said. "I just saw her in jeans for the first time recently. She looked so different."

"Different good or different bad?"

"Very good. She mostly wears skirts and suits to work."

Brooke even wore expensive-looking silky pajamas to bed, and I was very happy to peel them off her. Sometimes, she just climbed into bed naked to save me the trouble.

I liked those nights a lot.

We didn't always have sex. Some nights, she was exhausted from work, so we sat up in bed, watching terrible reality TV shows.

"I hope you don't mind," she'd said. "I watch three different shows. I can just turn my brain off and watch them."

"I don't mind," I said.

And I didn't. Because she'd snuggle against my side as I wrapped an arm around her and enjoyed the closeness. Sometimes, we ate ice cream or just talked. We had so much to talk about, and I loved learning more about her.

I found out she had taken ice skating lessons as a child. Her grandfather tapped trees for maple sap, then cooked it up into maple syrup for them to eat the rest of the year. She told me about her sister Megan.

My growing-up years weren't quite as wholesome, but I told her stories about Matty in happier times. Like birthday parties, swimming at the lake, and playing in the yard—simple, but fun.

I finished my glass of soda, smiling at the memory of a toothless Matty with dirt on his cheeks from playing in the yard.

"Can I get you another one?" Amanda asked.

"Nah." I took out my wallet and paid her. "Thanks."

"Have a fun night," she said. "And don't forget to tell her she's beautiful."

"I won't."

I went to the bathroom in the lobby, then sat on one of the plush benches that had a view of the staircase and the elevators. Finally, the elevator doors opened, and Julia walked out.

My heartbeat kicked against my ribcage as I watched for Brooke. A woman stepped out of the elevator, wearing a dark purple, floor-length gown with her hair tied up. When she put her hand to her neck and patted her necklace, I recognized the movement.

Brooke. Of course it was Brooke. There wasn't a dressy event at the hotel tonight.

She looked different again. Her dark hair was tied up in a way I hadn't seen before, and dangly earrings decorated her ears —Brooke usually wore small studs or small pearl earrings. Silver shoes peeked out beneath her hem as she walked toward me. She held a tiny silver purse.

Julia came toward me, grinning.

"Close your mouth, Evan, and tell her she's beautiful."

I clamped my mouth shut as Brooke walked up to me.

"Evan, wow. You look so handsome."

"Thanks. You look... you're so... beautiful."

"Thank you. Well, we should get going. Julia says the car is here."

"Car?" I asked stupidly. "I thought we were taking your car."

"No, Julia's arranged a car with a driver."

I looked over at Julia, who winked at me. I reached out and took Brooke's hand. As we walked past the restaurant, I saw Amanda standing close to the glass window, giving me a thumbs-up. I grinned at her.

A black sedan was parked right outside the door. The driver opened the door to the back seat. I let Brooke get in first, then I climbed in. The back seat was so roomy and comfortable. We settled in for the ride as the driver closed the door. The car pulled into the street, and we headed to the museum where the fundraiser was being held.

I took a closer look at Brooke's dress. It was sleeveless, and the front was decorated with little silver gemstones, and the fabric was soft and gathered at the waist.

Taking Brooke's hand, I held it up, placing a kiss on her fingers.

She smiled. "What was that for?"

"Thanks for picking me to squire you around, even though you made me wear a tux."

Brooke's laughter filled the car.

FIFTEEN

When we got out of the car, we saw other people heading in wearing formal clothing. I tugged at my collar, thinking I tied my bow tie too tight.

"Do you know where to go?" I asked.

"Yes. I've been coming to this fundraiser for years."

I wondered if she came to this thing with a boyfriend. We approached a table where people were checking in.

"Brooke Sinclair and Evan Handler," Brooke said.

"Hello, Miss Sinclair! Welcome back. Here's a program, and dinner will be held in the usual spot."

"Thank you."

Brooke led me through the tall, marble-floored lobby. She told me tonight was a fundraiser for the renovations for the hotel. There was a silent auction with donations from local businesses, plus the dinner. Tickets for the dinner were two hundred dollars each.

Several people milled around the tables, looking at the items up for auction.

"What kinds of things are up for auction?" I asked.

"Oh, the usual. A ski weekend in the mountains. A hotel for

the weekend in Boston. Minimum bids start at three hundred dollars."

Oof.

"Do you usually place some bids?" I asked.

"Yes, but I don't usually win them. That's okay, though."

Waitresses circulated with trays of champagne. Brooke took one, but I passed. I wasn't drinking *that* again.

"Oh, Diane will be here tonight," she said. "And some of the other people we met at the dinner party, like Linda and Charles."

She rolled her eyes. I got the feeling there was some tension between Brooke and Linda at the dinner party. I didn't know them that well, but it was good to know I'd see at least a few familiar faces.

We walked around and looked at the items up for auction, and Brooke bid on a few things. She bid on the ski weekend and the weekend in Boston.

"Do you ski?" I asked.

"No, but I've always wanted to learn. What about you?"

"No, we didn't have any money for that."

"Have you ever been to this museum?" Brooke asked.

"A couple of times, on school field trips. I'm afraid I don't know much about art."

"We could come here sometime and have a look around."

"I'd like that," I said.

"Brooke, is that you?" a woman asked.

We turned and saw Linda and Charles approaching. Linda's greying hair was tied up off her neck, and she was wearing a red gown.

"It is you! You look good in purple."

Linda gave Brooke air kisses while Charles shook my hand.

"Nice to see you again, Eric," he said.

"Evan," I said.

"Brooke, did you bid on anything yet?" Linda asked.

"I bid on the ski weekend, and the weekend in Boston."

"Oh, I think I'll go outbid you on that ski weekend," Charles said. "I like to win that one. We'll see you at dinner."

Brooke finished her champagne and handed the glass to a passing waitress. We walked into one of the museum rooms open for the event. The room held paintings from some of the European master painters.

Brooke had taken some art classes at college, so she told me what she knew about some of the paintings. I listened carefully, marveling at all the things she knew. She was so damn smart and accomplished, I still couldn't figure out why she was with a guy like me, who knew so little about the finer things in life.

But I wanted to learn. I wanted to go to the museum with her and learn more about art. I wanted to learn how to ski with her.

And most of all, I wanted to come home to her every single night, watch bad TV shows, and cuddle in bed. I wanted to reach for her every night and kiss her neck. I wanted to slip my hand into her pajama pants to get her wet for me.

"Brooke Sinclair!" a man said.

We turned and saw a man in a tuxedo. He had brown hair, chiseled cheekbones, and his tuxedo was fitted to perfection over his broad shoulders. He looked like a model.

"Stephen, hello!" Brooke said.

Stephen stepped forward and placed a kiss on Brooke's cheek, and it wasn't an air kiss. Heaviness lodged in my gut, especially with the way Stephen was undressing Brooke with his eyes.

"You look gorgeous in that color," he said.

"Thank you. Stephen, this is Evan Handler. Evan, Stephen Cummings."

I put out my hand, and Stephen grasped my fingers hard, making me wince.

"Good to meet you, Eric."

"It's *Evan*," I said through gritted teeth. How freaking hard was it to get my name right?

I decided I didn't like Stephen Cummings or his big, toothy smile. I didn't like the way he was mentally undressing Brooke or standing so close to her. I put a possessive hand on Brooke's hip.

"It's too bad you're here with someone," Stephen said as if I wasn't even standing next to him. "I thought we could sit together at dinner and maybe dance later."

"You don't have a date tonight?" Brooke asked.

"No, darling, you weren't available," he said, laughing.

Brooke opened her mouth, and I tried to shoot laser beams into her head with my thoughts. *Don't invite him to sit with us. Don't invite him to sit with us.*

"Come and find us at dinner," Brooke told him. "Linda and I usually sit at the same table every year."

"I know the one, darling," he said. "I need to go shake some hands. Later?"

Brooke nodded. Stephen took Brooke's hand and lifted it to his mouth for a kiss that lasted a few seconds too long.

The rat bastard.

"Who the hell was that?" I asked after he left.

"Stephen Cummings."

"I know, but who is he? Do you work with him?"

"No, I know him from some fundraisers for the hotel. His donation helped to renovate the hotel lobby."

"What is he, a model or something?"

"He used to model for a men's magazine."

I blinked at her. "Are you serious?"

"Yes. Why?"

"Is he still a model?"

"No. He manages his family's business and owns a jet charter company."

"Sounds like a real slacker," I joked.

Brooke smacked me on the chest with her purse. "Come on, let's go sit at our table. The food they serve for this event is amazing."

* * *

WE SAT AT OUR TABLE. Charles and Linda were there, and I ended up sitting between Brooke and Linda.

I surveyed the glass and silverware situation, going over each one in my head. A waiter came around and filled the water glasses. Stephen came over and sat next to Brooke. A few minutes later, Diane came over.

We all said hello. I waited for the others to take their napkins off their plates, then I did the same, making sure I didn't flop the fabric around.

The waiters came around with the first course. It was three small pieces of crusty bread covered with a light brown—was that a paste of some sort? It didn't look like the kinda thing you'd eat with a fork.

Linda picked up a piece of bread and took a bite, so I did the same.

"Oh, I just *love* chicken liver pâté!" Charles said.

As soon as he said that, I tasted the pâté and tried not to gag. It tasted very strange. I didn't like the smell or the texture, and it had an odd aftertaste. I looked at Brooke, who was nibbling an edge of her bread not covered in pâté.

Soon the waiters were clearing those plates and coming around with another plate. This course had tiny pieces of what looked like meat, covered in a thick white sauce. I took a small bite, and it wasn't bad, whatever it was.

Next came a tiny crock of soup that I couldn't quite identify. I only ate a little, since I had no idea how many courses were coming.

Stephen was leaning over, telling Brooke some story that made her smile. And then he put his hand on her arm. Just like the earlier peck on the cheek, his hand stayed there a bit too long for my liking. I shot him a look, but he ignored me.

The plates were removed, and a salad was brought out. This one wasn't wilted, though. It was ice cold, and so was the plate it was served on. The dressing was pretty good.

Next came what I guessed was the main course. It looked and smelled like salmon, but there was meat stuffed inside it.

I leaned toward Brooke, since Stephen was now talking to the man on his other side.

"What's this? It looks like salmon."

"Seafood-stuffed salmon fillets," she said.

Great. Just stuff fish inside another fish. I looked at my utensils. Damn, had I already used the wrong fork? Did this course mean I had to use the fish fork? Why did rich people need so goddamn much silverware?

I looked around, but couldn't tell who was using which fork, so I just picked up the next one and started eating. The fish was fine, since I didn't mind salmon. There was asparagus on the plate, and I ate some of that, too.

"Oh, I hope they have those lovely red velvet cakes again," Linda said. "Those are just to die for!"

"They are," Brooke said.

Red velvet cake was coming up. Okay, I could get on board with that.

"So, Evan, what do you do for work?" Stephen asked.

At least he got my name right this time.

"I'm an architect," I said. "Residential."

"He went to Cornell," Brooke said.

"Oh, really?" Stephen asked. "My brother went there. Were you in any fraternities?"

I swallowed a bite of salmon. "No, I wasn't. Too much studying to do."

"That's a shame," he said. "Were you in any clubs?"

Think, Handler. Think.

"I was in the chess club for a while," I said.

Beside me, Brooke was sitting very still.

"Oh, chess club! Was Professor Darby your club advisor?"

"Uhh..."

Shit. I was blowing it. Sweat trickled down my temple. Brooke opened her mouth, but she was interrupted.

"Attention, please. Could I have your attention, ladies and gentlemen?"

Someone was speaking into a microphone. Whatever he was about to say, I was grateful, because it saved me from answering any more questions.

The announcer talked about the museum and the fundraiser, thanking endless lists of volunteers. The waiters came around to take away the dinner plates.

Next, the winners of the silent auction were announced. The crowd politely applauded after each name was read. Charles won the ski weekend. And Brooke won the weekend for two in Boston.

"Yes!" she said.

Brooke slid her chair back and walked to the front of the room to collect her prize. Watching her walk away, I saw how every man in the place swiveled his head to watch her. In a sea of mostly black gowns, she stood out, so striking in her purple dress and dark hair.

Stephen leaned over toward me.

"This thing with you and Brooke, is it serious?"

"What?" I asked, not believing my ears.

"Dunno if you're just a friend or a guy from the office."

"No, I'm *not* just a friend or a co-worker. And yes, it's serious, so back off," I said.

He put his hands up. "Hey, no harm in trying."

Brooke was heading back to our table holding her envelope. Stephen slid back over to his chair as I stood to pull out Brooke's chair.

"Thank you, Evan. Wow, I can't believe I finally won this! I bid too much."

"When is it for?" Linda asked.

Brooke opened the envelope and pulled out a paper.

"It's for a weekend this summer. Maybe Evan can come with me."

"Sure," I said, not meeting her eyes.

I'd be long gone by summer, and I knew it. She'd go with some other guy. Maybe she could ask Stephen if she felt that way about him. The smug bastard.

"Oh, look, dessert is coming!" Linda said.

"Excuse me for a second," I said. "I need some air."

Brooke looked up at me, bewildered, as I headed for the exit.

SIXTEEN

I walked out to the lobby, and my phone rang. It was Matty. I slowed down a little, took a deep breath, and picked it up.

"Hey, Matty," I said.

"Hey, what's up? Sorry I haven't called in a while. I've been busy studying for some huge tests."

"No problem," I said. "I've been pretty busy myself."

"How's Operation Buy a House Coming?"

I sighed. "Well, it's going a lot better. Pretty soon, I'll have enough for a down payment. And I met a real estate agent who's going to show me some small houses."

"Don't worry about it," Matty said. "I won't mind if I have to crash on Liam's couch for a while. He's a lot of fun."

It was true. Liam practically rolled out the red carpet when Matty was around. He kept the place cleaner and cooked more. Matty was like the little brother Liam never had.

"Well, I'm really hoping you won't have to do that again. I'm real close to getting the rest of the money together."

"You're not doing anything illegal, are you?" Matty said, but I could hear the smile in his voice.

I headed out the doors, into the fresh air outside the museum, and took a deep breath of cool spring air.

"Nothing you need to know about," I joked, even though that was true.

"Okay. I gotta go, we're heading out for pizza."

"Okay, Matty. Take care of yourself."

"I'm doing good, Evan. I promise. Later, the guys are here."

He hung up, and I shoved my phone back into my pocket.

The museum door opened, and Brooke stepped out.

"There you are. I looked near the bathrooms, but I couldn't find you."

"Yeah. It was just getting stuffy in there, and this tie is bugging me."

I put my finger inside my tie and loosened it a little.

Brooke tilted her head. "Is everything okay? You seemed upset in there."

I rubbed the back of my neck, considering if I should tell her what Stephen said.

"I just—shit. I'll just say it. That guy, Stephen? He asked me if what you and I had was serious."

She crossed her arms. "And what did you say?"

"I told him yes, it was serious. And I told him to back off. But I'm just kidding myself. I have nothing to offer you. Not like Stephen."

She put her hand on my cheek. "Hey, that's not true."

"It is. Once I go to these next few events, we'll be done, and you can date Stephen. Or any guy here who probably has a tuxedo in his closet."

"Evan, I'm with you. Only you. I don't even like Stephen or any man here. I want to be with you."

Looking into her blue eyes, I wanted to believe her. She tugged my face down and pressed a firm kiss on my mouth.

"None of these men hold a candle to you. And I don't need

anything from you. In case you haven't noticed, I have my own money."

I grinned. That, she did.

"Now, come back in and try this red velvet cake, before Linda eats yours. Please?"

I took her hand, and we went back inside.

* * *

THE RED VELVET cake *was* incredible.

They had cleared out some of the tables, exposing a dance floor. A DJ playws music. Brooke was shimmying to the music by my side.

"Ask your girlfriend to dance before someone else does!" Linda shout-whispered in my ear.

I took Brooke's hand and led her to the floor where several people were dancing to the latest dance hit. Brooke was a good dancer. I felt like I was kinda flailing, but no one seemed to notice.

I finally loosened my tie and stuffed it into my pocket, giving my neck blessed relief. And when a slow dance song came on, I pulled Brooke into my arms. She rested her head near my shoulder. I loved the way her body felt next to mine. My chest ached, thinking about the end of our arrangement.

Brook sighed and hugged me. I hugged her back and kissed her cheek. She smelled so good tonight, like a different kind of flower.

The slow dance ended, and we went back to our table to drink some water. Stephen was still sitting there, his cake uneaten, glaring at me.

"Do you mind if we call it a night?" Brooke asked. "I have an early showing tomorrow."

"Not at all."

"I'll go out to the lobby and call for the car. It's too loud in here. Let me say goodbye to a few people first."

"Sure," I said.

She said goodbye to Stephen, who barely gave her a nod. And then she said goodbye to Linda and Charles.

"Goodbye, darling," Linda said. "I know duty calls."

I shook hands with Charles and let Linda give me an air kiss.

"Good night, Evan. Take care of our girl."

She winked, and I got an odd feeling from her. But then she walked away, and I followed Brooke out to the lobby.

* * *

BROOKE SNUGGLED against me in the back seat of the car. I opened the window a few inches to let in the cool night air. I leaned back against the seat and closed my eyes. Damn, I was tired, too.

When we got back to the hotel, the lobby was deserted. We headed toward the elevator.

"Hold on," Brooke said. "Do you mind if we stop by and see Charlie for a minute before we go up? I want to tell him I won the weekend in Boston. He knows I've been trying to win that."

"Sure," I said.

We walked past the desk and down the hallways to the bar. There were a few patrons drinking at tables. No one was sitting at the bar, but Charlie was there.

"Does this guy sleep here, too?" I asked, only half-joking.

"Ha, ha. Charlie, I won the weekend in Boston!"

We went up to the bar. Brooke opened her tiny purse and took out the envelope, which she'd rolled up to fit inside.

"Two nights in a suite, dinner included, and a gift certificate for a couples' massage."

"Hey, good!" he said. "It's about time you won that."

"I'm parched," she said. "Dinner was good but very salty. How about a quick drink before we go upstairs?"

"Sure," I said.

I knew she was tired, and I was, too, but I was so goddamned thirsty, I felt like I'd swallowed sand. Brooke ordered a white wine, then excused herself to go to the ladies' room. I ordered a beer. Charlie poured the wine and set it down on a coaster.

He poured my beer, and then set it down hard on a coaster, splashing some on my hand. He glared at me.

"Hey, Charlie. What the *hell* is your problem with me?"

He sighed and put his hands on the bar.

"I just see another rich asshole cozying up to Brooke, and I can just tell you're gonna break her heart."

I stared at him, stunned.

"What do you mean, I'm a rich asshole?" I asked. "Me? You've got the wrong idea, pal."

"I'm not your pal," he growled. "Did Brooke tell you about her ex?"

I thought for a second and remembered a conversation where I suspected she'd had a difficult past relationship.

"Not really. Why?"

"The last guy Brooke was with was a drunk, and he hit her. Did she tell you that?"

I felt like all the air was sucked out of my lungs. I blinked, then shook my head.

"No. She didn't."

"Well, you kinda remind me of him. It just don't sit right with me."

I sputtered. "Wh-What? So because I *look* like him, I'm doing the same thing, too? How the hell is that fair?"

Brooke came back, fanning her face. "It's hard to go to the

bathroom in this dress." She walked up to the bar and reached for her drink. She looked at Charlie, who was glaring at me.

"What's going on, here?" she asked. "Evan?"

"Charlie here just told me about your ex-boyfriend. The one you used to come in here with. Apparently, he thinks I resemble him, so I'm guilty by association."

Her posture went rigid, and she glared at him.

"Why did you tell him that?"

"I don't know, honey. I'm sorry. I'm just looking out for you, that's all."

"I can't believe this." She picked up her wine glass. "I'm going up to our room."

She turned to walk away.

"Brooke!" Charlie said, anguish on his features. "I'm sorry. I really am. I shouldn't have butt in. And you can't carry that through the lobby, I'll get in trouble."

She walked back to the bar and set the glass down hard, sloshing some wine over the edge. And then she turned and walked away. The patrons at the tables were watching us with interest. Brooke walked toward the door and went into the hall-way, out of sight.

"Shit. Here," I said, tugging out my wallet. "Let me pay for these—"

But Charlie was shaking his head and put his hand out.

"No, man. Don't worry about it. Go talk to her."

"Thanks," I said, and went after Brooke.

* * *

I MET her at the elevator, and we rode up to the room in silence. I opened the door with my key, and she went into the bedroom. She kicked off her shoes, then came back out.

"Can you unzip me, please?" she asked.

Her voice was quiet, and it unsettled me.

"Sure," I said.

She turned around, and I found the zipper, tugging it down to her waist.

"Thank you. I'm going to get changed."

She went into the bedroom. I heard fabric rustling, and a long sigh as she took off the dress. She hung it in the closet, and then she went into the bathroom and closed the door.

I paced back and forth, wondering what to do. Was she mad at me? At Charlie? At both of us?

Water ran in the bathroom. She was probably washing off her makeup, a nightly ritual. I went into the bedroom and took off my shoes and my tux, carefully hanging it up in the closet.

I peeled off my socks, then walked to the kitchen for a drink of water. I felt strange just standing around in my underwear, so I went into the bedroom and climbed into bed, waiting for her.

SEVENTEEN

Brooke stayed in the bathroom a long time, and when she came out, she was wearing pajamas and smelled like the face cream she applied before going to bed.

She set the alarm on her phone and climbed into bed.

I'd shut off the light in the kitchen. Only the bedside light was still on.

"Are you ready for me to turn out the light?" she asked.

"Yeah," I said.

She reached over and turned off the switch, settling into the mattress with her back to me. I didn't get the sense she was mad at me, but still, I wanted to tread carefully.

"Can I touch you?" I asked.

"Sure," she said.

I moved a little closer and draped my arm around her waist. She put her hand on mine.

"So, what was that about tonight?" I asked. "I'll listen if you want to talk about it. If not, that's okay, too."

She was quiet for so long, I thought she didn't want to talk and had started to fall asleep.

"I have terrible taste in men," she said. "Always have. I always think things are going great, and then..."

"And then?"

"And then they cheat. Or they only want me for my money. Or for my business connections. And the last one was a drunk, and he hit me."

I let all that sink in. "Well, you broke up with him."

"I made excuses. He only hit me when he was drunk. He just lost control, he won't do it again, I thought. I kept telling myself the same thing over and over. When he wasn't drunk, he was a great guy. Everyone loved him at work. No one suspected a thing. I was too embarrassed to tell anyone."

"None of it is your fault," I said.

"I know. I know that. Charlie saved me. He saw us at the bar one night. And my boyfriend—his name was Gabe—was drinking too much. Charlie refused to serve him anymore, and he got belligerent. He grabbed my arm really hard and dragged me out of there."

Silence. I waited until she was ready to talk again.

"Charlie looked up my name from a credit card receipt, and he found my address. He had one of the guys in the kitchen cover the bar for him, and he came to our apartment."

I pictured Charlie stalking up to the door and pounding on it like I'd pounded on Ray's door.

"When I looked out the peephole, I couldn't believe he was standing there. Gabe was in the bathroom, so I opened the door a crack and asked Charlie what he was doing there. Charlie told me to come out into the hallway and talk to him. I told him to leave. I opened the door a little more, and he put his hand on my arm, urging me into the hallway. I winced in pain."

A breath whooshed out of me.

"He told me to push up my sleeve *right now, damnit*. I tried to refuse, but he insisted. I pushed it up and showed Charlie the bruising that had already set in when Gabe tugged me out of the bar. I had older bruises of different colors on my arm, too."

My chest ached for Brooke. I *hated* guys who hit women.

"Charlie let go of my arm and closed the apartment door behind me. He told me to come with him. I didn't even have any shoes on! I walked out to his car with him. He told me to get in, and that he was calling the cops. I climbed in, and he locked the doors and closed them."

Now I was holding my breath, waiting for the rest of the story.

"Charlie picked up his phone and called the police. A few minutes later, Gabe came out to the parking lot looking for me. He was still drunk. Gabe walked over and talked to him. He pointed at his car, then pointed to his phone. Gabe started walking toward the car."

"Oh, shit," I said.

"Charlie said something to him, and Gabe turned around, swinging his fist. Charlie dodged the punch, and then he moved so fast, I couldn't see what he did, but he knocked Gabe to the ground and pinned him there. Gabe struggled and screamed at him, but Charlie didn't let him up until the cops arrived."

"Wow," I said.

"The cops put Gabe in the back of their car. And then they talked to Charlie for a few minutes. Charlie pointed to his car, and one of the cops came over to talk to me. He asked if I wanted to come down to the station and file a report. I said yes. He asked if anyone could give me a ride. Charlie said he would."

"I'm glad Charlie did that," I said.

"When he got into the car with me, he said his piece of shit brother-in-law used to hit his sister, and he knew a battered woman when he saw one. And Gabe's behavior had gotten increasingly worse from what he saw in the bar."

"What happened after that?"

"Gabe went to jail for a while. Then my sister and my friends brought me over to the apartment and helped me pack up all my stuff and move out. The apartment was in his name, anyway. I moved to a new one and resolved to never let something like that happen again."

"I'm sorry that happened to you, Brooke."

I kissed her shoulder and pulled her closer. She turned to face me.

"I brought you to the bar partly so Charlie could check you out. He's good at reading people. I called him the next day to ask his opinion of you, and he said he wasn't sure he liked you."

"Why?" I asked. "I've never treated you badly."

"I know. But Charlie said he sensed you weren't being completely honest about something."

"I'm a pretty open book," I said. "But there is something I haven't told you yet. I think it's time."

"What is it?"

My mouth felt dry again, and I swallowed hard.

"My dad used to hit our mom."

Brooke gasped. "Oh, Evan."

"He didn't drink. But he was so controlling about mom. He questioned what she did, where she was going. He accused her of cheating on him. He'd pick fights with her and lose control and smack her around at night when he thought me and Matty were asleep."

"But you heard them."

"Of course. We lived in a small house. We were just a few footsteps away, down the hall, listening to our mother cry."

Rage bubbled up in my throat again, thinking about how hopeless I felt. I was older than Matty, why didn't I *do* something? But our dad was tall and muscular. All he had to do was glare at us, and we'd behave.

"Did he hit you or your brother?"

"No," I said. "He never did. I always thought he'd come storming down the hallway and smack us around, but he never did. Matty used to sneak into my room when they fought. I'd let him climb into bed with me. He'd shake in fear. I used to get up and sit with my back against the door to make sure dad didn't come in and hurt us. Our doors didn't have locks, and I'm sure dad could've pushed in the door if he really wanted to."

I remember nights lying by the door and trying to fall asleep on the dingy carpet. Matty used to bring me a pillow and blanket, and then he'd climb back into my bed and curl up, crying himself to sleep.

"One morning, I woke up by the door with a crick in my neck. I got up and went over to my bed to check on Matty. I pulled down his cover, and he was sleeping, clutching his stuffed monkey and sucking his thumb like a baby. He had dried tears on his cheeks, running back into his hair."

"Oh my God," Brooke said.

"I swore right then I was going to do something. I was going to skip school and go to the police."

"What happened?"

"I chickened out. What if the cops came, and they didn't arrest him? What if he blamed us and started hitting us? What if he took it out on mom? Matty begged me to do something every day. I didn't know what to do."

"You were just a kid," she said. "And then what?"

"Then, about a week later—I shit you not—Dad collapsed at work and died."

Brooke sucked in a breath.

"They called an ambulance, but they couldn't revive him. I told you about when my mom came to school to tell me he died, remember? And then we went to Matty's school to tell him. Matty was distraught. Even though we hated dad, he was so upset. Matty said it was all his fault because he'd wished out loud that Dad would die."

"Oh, Evan, I'm so sorry."

She put her hand on my cheek and kissed me on the lips. I kissed her back, threading my hands through her hair, trying to put so much into the way I held her and kissed her.

I'd never told anyone the full story, except for the counselor mom made me see after. I totally blamed dad for Matty getting into drugs when he got older. I was still bitter about it.

Brooke yawned. "Oh, I'm so sorry! I didn't mean to do that."

"No, it's okay. I'm exhausted, too. Let's get some sleep."

I held Brooke and stroked her hair until her breathing told me she was asleep, and then I quickly fell asleep, too.

EIGHTEEN

The next morning, Brooke's alarm woke us up. I moaned, and she rolled over, grabbing her phone and turning it off.

"Ugh," I said. "It can't be morning already."

"Mmm," she said.

She reached down, feeling my morning wood. We kissed, and she slipped beneath the covers and tugged down my underwear. Her soft hand slipped me into her warm mouth. I moaned —what a way to start the day.

Brooke teased me with her lips and tongue until I grew hard again. A few minutes later, she pulled away and tugged off her pajamas. When she came back to me, her pussy was wet. I grabbed a condom from the bedside table and handed it to her. I loved watching her tear it open and roll it down on me.

She straddled me, lifting herself up, and then slowly lowering herself onto my cock. I reached up and cupped her breasts as she moved above me. I loved the way she moved, and the little gasping sounds she was making.

A few minutes later, I reached out and rubbed her clit with my thumb. She moved faster on me, gasping and moaning. Her clit swelled under my touch. She pulled my hand away and ground hard on my cock. I bit my bottom lip, trying to hold off.

Everything faded away as she rode me—all I saw and felt and wanted was Brooke. Only Brooke. I wanted to sleep next to her every day. I wanted to make her coffee every morning. I wanted to come home and kiss her at the end of a long day.

"Oh Evan! I'm so close."

I grabbed her hips, helping her grind her clit against me, and she suddenly came, squeezing my cock until I exploded. She rode me until she finished, crying out and pulsing and squeezing my shaft.

And then she collapsed on my chest, panting.

I wrapped my arms around her and closed my eyes. We were just two broken people, coming together and trying to feel whole.

Our two weeks were coming to an end. I didn't want to lose her, but if she wanted a clean break, I'd give it to her.

"Evan?"

"Mmm?"

"I love you."

I sucked in a breath. "I love you, too."

She kissed me, and I held her so tight against my chest, I didn't ever want to let go.

* * *

I WAS sluggish all morning at work. I went back to the coffee pot in the break room way more than usual. By lunchtime, I had pretty much come out of my fog. I ate with the guys, and then I brought my mop and bucket out to the lobby to mop. It was raining outside, and people had been tracking in dirt and water all morning.

I was halfway through mopping when I heard some raised voices.

"That's not good enough!"

"Sir, please lower your voice."

"Incompetence! Complete and utter incompetence!"

I knew that voice.

Brad. That asshole.

I put my mop into my bucket and rolled it to the wall. Then I walked through the lobby and over to the desk. Carly was standing there scowling as Brad shouted at her.

"Hey," I said. "Simmer down, Brad. You're out of line!"

Carly looked relieved to see me.

Brad, however, was not.

"Don't tell me to simmer down! This woman lost my package. She's incompetent!"

"I haven't received a package for him in days," she said. "I checked the list. I checked the package closet. Nothing."

"Walk away," I told him, getting close to his face. "She doesn't have it."

His face turned red, then purple.

"The building manager will be getting a phone call from me."

"Good," I said. "You can tell her that you harassed the staff here, and she'll take our side and kick *you* out, I assure you."

I barely knew the building manager and had no idea if she'd stick up for us, but it worked. He straightened his blazer, then stalked out to the lobby and left.

"He's gone," I said, and Carly let out a long sigh of relief. "Do me a favor? Let me know when you get a package for him. I want to deliver it myself."

"Thank you, Evan," she said. "I owe you one."

"No problem," I said.

I finished mopping the lobby, then helped Frank change

some light bulbs. Half an hour before my shift ended, I was touching up some paint in a hallway when Carly called me on the radio.

"Evan? Can you come down here when you get a moment? That package is here."

I picked up my radio and answered. "I'll be down in ten."

After I finished touching up the paint, I brought my supplies down to the maintenance room and put them away. Carly was smiling when I went over to her desk.

"Here it is," she said. "It just came about fifteen minutes ago. Thanks for offering to do this so I don't have to."

"Got it."

I picked up the small box and carried it to the elevator. I was practicing what I was going to say to Brad on the ride up. When I reached his door, I knocked and braced myself.

He opened the door a few seconds later. I held the box up.

"Here's your package. Carly said it came fifteen minutes ago."

He reached for it, but I pulled it back.

"Listen, you can't talk to people that way. It's rude as hell, and if you want to get along with the building staff, this isn't the way to do it."

He looked down. "Alright."

I shoved the package in his hands and started walking away

"Evan?"

I stopped and looked back. "Yeah?"

He opened the door a little more. "I apologize. I've had a really tough week, and I've been awful."

Wow.

That wasn't what I was expecting to hear.

"Okay, but you really need to apologize to Carly."

"I will," he said, and he closed the door.

I walked back to the elevator, shaking my head.

* * *

THAT NIGHT, I headed over to Cooper's for another few games in our dart tournament. Liam was all wound up when I got there.

"Drew's half in the bag already, so he'll suck. And we just need to win two games tonight to advance to the semi-finals."

I nodded, checking my phone. "Yup."

Brooke had sent me a text earlier, and I was responding.

"Hey. Are you paying attention?"

"Huh? Yeah, sorry. I am. Drew's half-drunk already."

I shoved my phone in my back pocket and tried to pay attention to Liam. It was noisy as hell in the bar tonight, and crowded with all the guys here for the dart tournament. I lifted my beer to my lips and took a sip.

Liam sat back in his chair and shook his head.

"Man, you've got it bad for this girl. You're not even excited about tonight."

"Sorry about the phone, but you've got my full attention now. We're going to kick their asses. We've been practicing."

"*I've* been practicing. You've been gallivanting around in a tuxedo."

"Hardly."

"Look at you tonight. You're not even wearin' jeans! We're in a bar!"

I looked down at my dress pants and blue button-down shirt.

"So?"

"Well, you clean up real nice. It's just strange, seeing you all dressed up like this."

The guys had all whistled and laughed when I walked in wearing my nice clothes. They were all wearing their usual grubby and paint-stained work clothes and jeans. I'd raised my middle finger to the room and ordered a beer from Jenna.

"So, how's it going with her?" Liam asked.

"It's going well."

"Did she give you the money yet?"

I looked away. "No."

"Then it's not going so hot, is it?"

"She's gonna pay me."

"Uh huh. Did you sign a contract?"

"Well, no, but—"

"That's what's wrong with her. She's gonna stiff you, and then you won't have your down payment."

"She's not like that, Liam. She's gonna pay me."

"Well, I'll believe it when I see it." A roar went up, and the guys cheered and clapped. "Get ready, we're up next."

Liam went first and got a high score, but I choked.

"Shit," I said.

Our turn ended, but when I was up again, I did better, and we just won by a point.

"Damn, that was a close one," I said.

"No kiddin'. We gotta practice a lot before the semi-finals, okay?"

"Yeah, I know."

We sat down at our table again. My phone beeped, and I fished it out of my pocket. I read a text, grinned, and then put it back.

"That was Brooke. She said she left her hair thingy in my truck. I need to give it back to her. She likes to have her hair up when she goes to bed."

Liam was bringing his beer bottle up to his lips and paused.

"Oh, no," he said.

"What?"

"Oh, shit. This is terrible. You've fallen in love with her."

"What? No. I'm just talking about a hair thingy."

"No. I've seen that dopey look on your face before. You love this girl."

"She's not a girl, Liam. She's a woman. And yes, I care about her."

Liam took a swig of his beer. "Okay. Remember what I said, though. It just never works out between a woman like that and a guy like us."

We finished our beer, and I took out some cash and put it on the table.

"Here, that'll cover our bill. I gotta run."

Liam turned to me as I stood. "Just be careful, okay? I hate to see you get hurt."

"I know what I'm doing. I'll see you soon."

"Sure," he said, turning back to his beer.

I hated to see him sitting alone like that, but I knew the other guys would notice I left, and they'd draw him into their conversation.

When I left the bar, I stood outside on the sidewalk looking in for a minute. The bar's lights were dim, but I could see the peeling paint on the walls through the grubby windows. I could almost smell the dank bathroom from out on the sidewalk.

I walked away, knowing Brooke was just humoring me coming to the bar, and that she was used to nice, clean places where your shoes didn't stick to the floor.

But in less than a week, I'd stop seeing the insides of nice restaurants and hotel suites. I didn't care about the nice restaurants or the hotel suite, but about the woman who belonged in them.

NINETEEN

The rest of the week passed quickly. I got my tux back from the dry cleaner for the awards ceremony.

On Saturday, Brooke and I sat at the table in the suite eating breakfast.

"Are you wearing that same purple dress tonight?"

"No," she said. "I have a red dress for tonight."

"I'm wearing the same thing."

"Yes, but women can't get away with that. Especially since the fundraiser is so close to this ceremony."

The awards ceremony was a big deal for Brooke. She was up for Agent of the Year, and she was receiving an award for top sales in the region. The event was put on by a real estate association Brooke belonged to, and it was being held at the newly renovated ballroom at the hotel.

"What should we today?" she asked.

"Dunno. How long do you need to get ready for tonight?"

"Not as long. I won't need Julia to help me since I'm wearing a much simpler dress and hairstyle."

"I can help zip you," I said, wiggling my eyebrows.

She laughed. "I'm not sure how you feel about this, but

there's a new kitchen store downtown I want to check out. I could use some new pots and pans."

"I don't mind," I said.

Half an hour later, we walked into the kitchen store. There were rows and rows of colorful cookware, dishes and kitchen tools. Brooke spent several minutes comparing the pots and pans, but I didn't mind. I was just happy to spend time with her.

"I really like this one," she said. "What do you think?"

She handed me a small pot with a lid. It was heavy as hell, and the price tag said ninety-five dollars.

"Ninety-five dollars? For *one* pan?" I asked.

"It's a good brand. Very high quality."

I handed it back to her. "Are you going to buy them today?"

"No, because I don't want to lug a huge box back to the hotel. I'll order them once I move back into my condo."

"Oh, I saw the workers going in to work on your carpet. Frank let them in. I like the color you chose."

"Thanks. You'll have to stop by and see it."

I stuffed my hands into my pockets. I wasn't sure how I could go into Brooke's condo without a work order. I didn't want any of the guys to see me.

"Sure," I said.

We spent some time window shopping, then went into a bookstore. The day was sunny and getting warmer, so we bought subs at a sandwich shop and brought them over to a small park with two picnic tables.

Brooke's hair blew in the wind. Flowers were starting to bloom, and the breeze had a fresh scent.

"I like this," I said when we finished eating.

"Me, too."

She reached across the picnic table and held my hand. Her phone rang.

"Damn," she said. "I should take this. I told my team I was taking the day off."

"Go ahead. Take it."

She took the phone call, and then we slowly walked back to the hotel. We talked on the way back, and I looked at our reflection in the glass fronts of shops we passed.

We looked so normal, like a boyfriend and girlfriend out on a normal day.

When we got back to the hotel, Brooke opened her laptop and checked her email.

"I got an email from the carpet installer," she said. "The carpet is finished."

My heart sank, but I knew they had to finish it eventually.

"Oh, and I've made a list of some homes to show you. I can email the listings to you, but I printed them at work."

She handed me a folder.

"They're in your price range. One is a little higher, but I think we can get it for a lower price since it needs some work."

I shuffled through the papers, looking at square footage and prices.

"Thanks, I'll take a look at these."

Brooke went to the kitchen to get a drink. A few minutes passed, and Brooke's computer screen turned to a screen saver. It was an enormous white house with black shutters and a red door. The front lawn was perfectly manicured, with decorative, trimmed shrubs.

"That's a nice house," I said, nodding at her computer. "That one you're selling?"

"No."

"It looks like one of those houses over on Lilac or Greenbriar."

She came over and sat next to me on the couch.

"That's my parents' house in Connecticut. That's my childhood home."

I turned and stared at her.

"That's where you grew up?"

"Yes." She closed her laptop. "I didn't mean for you to see that."

"Why not? Did you have a butler?" I joked.

She sighed. "Because of questions like that. People make assumptions about you."

"Sorry," I said.

"It's okay. My parents are both lawyers, and they have family money they've inherited. That's how I was able to afford the schools I went to. Private high school. Ivy league college."

"Yeah, I know all about people making assumptions. You should have seen the way those salesmen looked at me in the suit store when I went in wearing my work uniform."

"I'm so sorry about that. Julia told me about it."

"There's a guy that lives on the sixth floor on your building. He's a real asshole to the staff, especially Carly, who sits at the desk."

"Yes, I know Carly."

"He was rude to me, too. He seems to think we're his personal staff to order around. I had enough, and I called him on it. He finally apologized."

"People make a lot of assumptions based on appearance. It's not right, but we all do it."

That was something to think about. I had pre-judged Brooke, and so had Liam, just as people made judgments about guys like me and Liam.

"Do you remember Diane thanking me for helping with the renovations at the Carlisle?" she asked.

"Yeah, I was wondering about that."

"I gave the hotel a donation, and told my parents about it.

They sent in a donation for triple the amount I gave. I just didn't want to make a big deal about it."

That made sense. I leaned over and kissed her, pushing her down on the couch.

"You like having a grungy maintenance man kissing you, don't you?"

I tickled her and made her shriek, which dissolved into more kissing and tickling and laughter.

* * *

LATER THAT NIGHT, I headed to the main hotel bar again. Since it was a Saturday night, the restaurant and bar were a little more crowded, but I found a seat at the bar. Amanda was there again.

"Hey, handsome!" she said. "Getting some more wear out of that tux, I see."

"Yeah, another event tonight. She's got a different dress this time."

"I'll have to look and see when she comes down. What can I get you?"

I ordered another soda, and a while later, she texted me that she was coming down. I tossed some bills on the bar.

"Thanks, Amanda. She's coming down now."

"Okay. I'll watch for her."

"I will. They're having the event in the ballroom tonight."

"Oh, that's right, that's tonight! That explains why I've been seeing tuxedos and nice dresses tonight. Have fun!"

I walked into the lobby and waited for the elevator to come down. When it opened, she came out, and several people stopped to stare at her as she walked toward me. She wore a fitted red knee-length dress and silver heels. The top of her dress was off the shoulder with short sleeves. Her dark hair was straight and sleek, and I felt a rush of warmth, affection, and lust for her.

"Hi," she said.

"You look so beautiful."

"Thank you. Ready?" she asked.

I realized we weren't going to pass the bar, so Amanda wouldn't be able to see her.

"Hold on," I said. "Can we just step over here for a minute?"

I took her hand and led her over to the entrance of the bar. I waved at Amanda, and one of the patrons told Amanda to look up. She did, and gave us a wide smile and started applauding. I did a ridiculous bow and put my arm around Brooke. Some of the patrons laughed, and I heard scattered applause from the bar.

"What's all this about?" Brooke asked.

"I'll tell you later."

In the lobby, we saw more people dressed up and heading for the ballroom. Inside, they had an easel displayed with a list of tonight's dinner menu.

"Looks good," I said. "I can even pronounce most of those words. But I don't think I've ever had a croquette. Is that something I'll like?"

"Probably," she said.

The ballroom had been divided into a slightly smaller room with round tables set for dinner. We barely took a few more steps when Diane came up to us.

"Brooke, Evan. How nice you look!"

We spoke with her for a few minutes, then made our way to a table. Thankfully, the silverware situation was a little more under control at this event.

The scent of cooked food was making my stomach growl. Waiters came around to get drink orders.

"Linda, over here!" Diane said, waving.

Brooke let out an aggravated sigh, but before I could wonder about it, Linda and Charles came over to our table, and Linda sat by me. Tonight, she was wearing a blue dress with a deep neckline.

"We meet again, darling," she said.

"Nice to see you, Linda."

Waitresses came out with trays holding salads. Brooke and her coworkers talked shop a little. Then they talked about the hotel renovations. The conversation turned to food when the main course came out.

Dinner was excellent, especially the potato croquettes. Soon after dinner was cleared away, the awards ceremony began. We listened to some speeches, and I clapped when the others clapped. Finally, some of the awards were announced, and people went up to collect them.

Brooke was called up for her top sales award, and our table erupted in loud applause. She came back smiling, holding another wooden plaque to hang on the wall at work.

She didn't win the bigger award, and I patted her on the back.

"Oh well," she said. "Where's that waiter? I need another drink now."

"I'll get another one for you. Same thing?"

"Yes, thank you."

"I'll come with you," Linda said, standing up with me.

"Okay," I said.

We headed over to the bar in the corner of the room. There was a short line, so Linda and I stood together waiting. I looked over toward our table, but there were people and waitresses walking around, and I couldn't see Brooke from here.

"I'm so glad we got away for a little bit," Linda said. "I was hoping to ask you something."

I got a weird vibe from her again, and she was standing a little too close for my liking.

"Oh?" I asked, taking a small step back.

"Yes." She stepped closer again, turning her back to the room.

"Brooke told me that she hired you to be her escort for a couple of weeks. And I was wondering…"

She slipped her hand inside my jacket, touching my waist.

"I was wondering if you wanted a little extra work? Brooke said you're *very* discrete."

TWENTY

My mouth dropped open, and heat rushed up my neck and into my cheeks. I couldn't believe what I was hearing.

Brooke? Brooke told her about me?

I took Linda's hand and pushed it away.

"I don't know what Brooke told you, but it's not like that."

"Oh. Right." She winked. "I get it."

"No, I mean it. It's not what you think. Besides, aren't you married? Charles—"

"My husband has had a *special friend* for years now. And I'm looking for a new one. What do you say, Evan?"

"Sir, can I help you?" the bartender asked.

I walked up and ordered another drink for Brooke since I wasn't sure what else to do. I stuffed some money in the tip glass and waited, sweat running down my temple.

"Come now, darling," Linda said. "We're all adults. Won't you reconsider?"

The bartender came back with Brooke's drink, and I thanked him.

"It's not like you have better offers," Linda said. "Being a *janitor* is beneath a handsome man like you. You clean up quite nicely. I'm sure you could get more of... this type of work if you *really* wanted it. I have some friends who would be interested, too."

I picked up Brooke's drink and stormed back to the table, not caring that I was splashing wine on my tux. I had to wait for several waitresses to walk by. I finally reached the table and set Brooke's drink down in front of her, sloshing it on the white tablecloth.

"Here's your goddamn drink, Brooke. I'm leaving."

Brooke looked at me, her mouth open. "Evan, what's wrong?"

But I shook my head, turned, and stormed toward the exit. I weaved around tables and finally made it out into the hallway. I walked to the elevators, punching the up buttons on both of them.

I paced back and forth while the world's slowest elevators stopped on every floor. One of the elevators had come down to the second floor and stopped for over a minute.

"Come on!" I said, willing it to come down. "Come on!"

"Evan."

I heard Brooke's voice and saw her rushing toward me. The elevator doors opened, and I went inside, frantically pushing the button to close the door.

"Evan, please, I'm so sorry!" Brooke's cheeks were red, and tears ran down her cheeks, smearing her mascara. "Evan, wait!"

But the doors closed before she could reach me.

* * *

UPSTAIRS, I took off my tux and changed. I opened my bag and swept all my stuff from the bathroom counter in. I stuffed my jeans and t-shirts into my bag but left the dressy clothing in the bedroom.

I wasn't going to need it again.

I was stuffing my feet back into my sneakers when the door opened, and Brooke swept in, breathless and tear-stained.

"Evan. Please. The elevator took so long. Please. I can explain."

She was clutching her side, leaning over and gasping for air as if she'd run from the elevator and down the hall.

My insides clenched seeing her, but my anger overruled any romantic feelings I had.

"You made me feel so cheap tonight. Like a goddamn prostitute!" I said, trying not to yell. "I'm leaving. I'm so fuckin' embarrassed."

"Evan. Please."

"You told Linda about our deal, huh? Told her I was a *janitor*? Did you also tell Stephen? Did you tell Diane, and everyone else at the office? Have a laugh at my expense?"

"No, that's not what happened. I can explain!"

"Forget it," I said. "I'm leaving. I won't talk to you when I'm at work. And don't talk to me when you see me, either."

"I have your money," she said in a small voice. "I was going to give it to you tonight."

She walked over to the safe in the suite and punched in the combination. She took out a large envelope, then closed the safe. She walked over and laid the envelope on the small table.

"It's all there. You can count it. Please let me explain."

I shook my head. "No. I'm leaving."

Hoisting my bag over my shoulder, I scanned the room to see if I forgot anything. I saw my keys on the counter behind Brooke. I walked toward her and reached out for them, and she flinched, throwing up her hands and shielding her face.

Instantly, I felt like an asshole.

"Brooke, I'm so sorry. I was just reaching for my keys behind you."

She stepped aside, and I grabbed my keys and walked toward the door.

"I'm sorry, Brooke. I'd never hurt you. I've never raised a hand to a woman, and I never will."

"I know that," she said. "I just reacted, I couldn't help it. But please, take the money. I want you to get a house for you and Matty. I don't care if you use another agent to buy a house, just please do it. I'm so sorry."

She started sobbing and walked into the bedroom. I heard the bathroom door close, and her sobs became muffled.

I looked at the envelope on the table. So close.

But I couldn't take it. Not now.

I opened the door and left.

* * *

LIAM WAS DRINKING a beer and watching a movie when I got home. He sat up and paused the movie.

"Hey, what the hell are you doing here? Is the time up already?"

"It is now," I growled.

"Uh oh."

I went to my room and started unpacking my bag. Liam got up and came over to my doorway.

"You wanna talk about it?" he asked. "I can get you a beer."

"Maybe later. I want to take a shower and start some laundry."

"Okay. Well, just holler."

I took a shower, washing off the nice cologne Brooke had given me. After I got dressed, I grabbed my laundry basket and quarters and went down to the basement laundry room.

Thankfully, the laundry room was empty, but two of the dryers were on. I tossed my stuff in a washer, added my quarters, and turned it on. I debated staying down here with the hum of the machines for a while, but I trudged up the stairs and went back to the apartment.

Liam's movie was almost over. I went to the fridge and opened it to see what we had. Nothing looked appealing.

"Do we have any ice cream?" I asked.

"Yeah, I bought some this week."

I opened the fridge, took out the tub, and put it on the counter. I grabbed two bowls and two spoons. I picked up the carton and looked at the flavor.

Cookie dough.

"Shit."

"What?" Liam asked. "There should be some left."

"There is, it's just... it's Brooke's favorite flavor."

"Damn, I'm sorry. You told me to just get what was on sale."

"Yeah."

Opening the carton, I spooned some out for me and Liam, then threw the empty carton in the trash. I brought the bowls over to the couch, and we watched the rest of the movie.

"I rented this other movie," he said, clicking the remote. It was the newest action movie starring Liam's favorite actor. "Wanna watch it?"

"Sure," I said, settling into ice cream and a mindless movie.

I tried to concentrate on the plot and tried not to think about Brooke. An hour later, I checked my phone for messages. My heart leaped when I saw one from Brooke.

I love you.

I sighed and put my phone down. When the movie ended, I went down to swap my clothes to the dryer. When I came back up, Liam was sitting at the table.

"Okay, spill it. I can't deal with you moping around. Tell me what happened."

I sat down and started talking. I told him everything, and he shook his head or nodded at certain points. When I told him what Linda did, he sucked in a breath.

"Wow," he said when I finished. "Wow."

"That's all you've got?"

Liam raised an eyebrow. "Don't you think you were a *little* harsh? You aren't, in fact, a real gigolo. As much as you tried to be."

"I'm well aware."

"Can't you just avoid this Linda? Who cares if she thinks you're a gigolo?"

"Brooke violated my trust. I thought we had something real. Something good. And she goes around telling people at work that she hired someone to go to events with her?"

"First of all, you don't know if she told everyone."

"Liam—"

"You don't! Also, who keeps texting you?"

I slid my phone out of my pocket and looked at my messages.

Brooke.

Liam grabbed my phone out of my hand.

"Hey, asshole, give it back!"

"No way, I need to read these messages." He cleared his throat, then read Brooke's messages in a poor imitation of a woman's voice. "Evan, please talk to me. I love you. I'm so sorry, please let me explain."

I put my head in my hands.

"Wait a second. You two said, 'I love you'?" Liam asked. "Hoo boy."

"You wouldn't understand," I said.

"Oh, I understand. You think I've never said 'I love you' to a woman before?"

"I know you have."

"Talk to her. Please. I can see how much you care about her.

And I saw how she looked at you that night you brought her to the bar. She's nuts for you."

"I just need some more time."

"Don't take too much time. A woman like that won't stay single for long."

"A woman like that can get a guy with a better paying job who doesn't mop up other people's messes," I said. "In fact, you're the one who told me this would never work out, that we're too different."

"And you're listening to my advice? Look around, do you see me with a girlfriend? No. Give her a chance. Find out why she ratted on you. If you don't at least talk to her, you're dumber than I thought."

TWENTY-ONE

I texted Brooke back later that night, asking her to please give me more time, and that I'd call her soon. She thanked me, then stopped texting.

I went through Monday at work like a zombie. I had to do some work on Brooke's floor. I hurried through it, anxious to finish, but her door never opened. I wasn't sure if she had moved back in yet.

Before the end of the day, I went over to Carly's desk.

"Carly, have you seen Brooke Sinclair around today?"

"Brooke Sinclair. Oh yes—she just had new carpets installed. I don't think she's come back just yet. I haven't seen her, but maybe I missed her."

"Okay, thanks."

I went back to the break room and packed up my stuff to leave. I said goodbye to Frank and went out to my truck. When I got inside the cab, I pulled out my phone and texted Brooke.

Can we meet soon? I just got out of work.

I waited an agonizing minute, then she texted back.

Yes. I have a showing at four-thirty near downtown. Meet me at the picnic table where we ate lunch at 5:30?

I agreed and said I'd see her then.

I had some time to kill, but I really didn't want to go back to our apartment, which was in the opposite direction. I started my truck and drove toward downtown. I parked and decided to take a walk.

The sun was out, and the temperature had reached seventy. I lifted my face to the sun. Birds chirped in the trees, and flowers bloomed. I took the long way, walking down a couple of streets with houses I liked.

The big brick home on the corner with a wide front porch looked like a home Brooke would sell. The old stone house with green shutters that had a tangle of bushes and tall grass in the yard and looked neglected. And the next street over, the grey ranch with flower boxes at the windows and kids' toys in the yard.

I slowed down when I saw a For Sale sign in the ranch's front yard. No way. It was finally for sale! I stopped and looked at the windows, and the roof. It was probably built in the fifties, but it looked solid and well-kept. It had large windows that would make the interior sunny. I started walking again and peeked into the back yard. There was a swingset back there, and more plastic kids' toys.

It looked like a great house for a family with kids. Maybe someday I'd have that. I took my phone out and snapped a picture of the agent's number on the For Sale sign. Then I took a picture of the house.

When I got to the park, it was five-thirty. I walked around, looking for Brooke. A mom and two kids were sitting at our picnic table, but they got up and left after a few minutes.

I sat down at the table and waited.

God, I missed Brooke's smile. I missed her touch. I missed falling asleep next to her. I missed eating dinner with her.

I didn't have a plan about what to say. I had imaginary conversations with her, but everything sounded wrong.

Ten minutes passed. Where was she?

I was looking down at my feet when I heard heels clicking on the sidewalk. Brooke! I grinned and stood up immediately. She was rushing toward me in a navy blue suit and pearls. She had on giant sunglasses, and her dark hair blew in the wind.

"Evan, I'm so sorry I'm late! My showing took so long."

I walked over to meet her, and we both stopped a few feet apart. My hands ached to touch her, to pull her into my arms and run my fingers through her soft hair. To make her come, while she cried out, digging her nails into my back.

"Hi," I said. "You look nice."

"Thank you. Should we sit down?"

"Sure."

We sat side by side on the bench, and she lifted her sunglasses on top of her head. She had makeup on, but it looked like she was trying to conceal dark circles under her eyes. I knew how she felt; I hadn't gotten much sleep, either.

"Brooke, I just want to say again that I'm so sorry I made you flinch that day. I felt so awful about that."

"I could tell."

Silence fell, but I sat with it for a minute.

"I'd never hurt you. I saw what my mom went through and swore up and down I'd never be like my dad."

She nodded.

"I never got into fights at school like the other boys. I just couldn't stand fighting, even just shoving matches between kids in the schoolyard. Matty, too. He's had problems with drugs, but he never got violent."

There was so much I wanted to say, I didn't know where to start.

"You can ask my roommate, my friends. The guys in the

maintenance department. I don't lose my temper like that. Well, except for when Matty left rehab. Mom and I drove around looking for him, and I threatened his friend and pushed him against the wall, but Matty wasn't there."

"I believe you. Julia also looked to see if you had an arrest record, remember?" She gave me a tiny smile. "By the way, I told Julia that you were a friend when I enlisted her to help me and assist you if you needed it. She didn't question it."

"Okay."

"Linda, on the other hand. I can't stand that woman. She's always been out to get me."

"Really? You hid it pretty well at the dinner and at the fundraiser."

"I have to tolerate her, we're a small office."

"What happened? How did she find out?"

Brooke sighed. "It's all my fault. Linda said she suspected you didn't actually go to Cornell. Her sister works in the alumni office there."

"Uh oh."

"I totally forgot about that. I did look into going there, though. Anyway, her sister looked up your name on the list of alumni, and—"

"Oh, no."

"She found your name, but it belonged to a man who graduated in sixty-eight. Obviously not you. Then she went into my office when I was at lunch. She snooped around and found a file on my desk. I had the results of your background search in there. This was after the dinner at Diane's. She kept quiet for a few days. Then she cornered me in my office at the end of the day after everyone else had left. She told me she'd seen the file on you, and she asked me why I was looking up info about you."

"Unbelievable."

"I didn't want to tell her about Gabe. That all happened

before I started working at Turner. I just said that I was being cautious because I met you on a dating site. But then she asked me why I had a bank withdrawal receipt for ten thousand dollars in that folder. She asked if I had hired a... you know."

"A male escort?"

"I lied and said no. She threatened to tell everyone at work. I begged her not to. I told her I took out some cash to pay for my new carpets, but she didn't believe me. She liked torturing me, holding it over my head."

"Wow."

"I asked her what she wanted in return for her silence. Even though I knew I hadn't done anything wrong, I was afraid she'd ruin my reputation at work, and possibly tell other agents around town. And in this business, it's all about reputation."

She stopped talking and watched a yellow butterfly go by.

"Linda told me she wanted the house on Lilac. I was furious! I had built a relationship with that seller over the years. I loved that house. I had sold it to him and told him to keep me in mind when he sold again, and he did. The owner put in a new kitchen, new bathrooms, refinished the hardwood floors. Housing prices just kept going up, and I knew the house would sell for a fortune."

"So, you gave it to her."

"Yes. I shouldn't have. Linda still had my secret hanging over my head. Every time I disagreed with her at a meeting, she'd tilt her head and shoot me a look, like she was about to spill the beans."

"Oh, man."

"After the awards ceremony, I couldn't stand it anymore. I asked Diane for a private meeting in her office. I told Diane that I'd hired you, that I was paying you to accompany me to these events because I hated going to them alone."

"What did she say?"

"She was quiet for several seconds, and then she burst out laughing!"

"What?"

"I was so angry and embarrassed, but Diane said 'I apologize, dear, but it's really very funny. Why on *earth* would you pay a man to escort you to events when you could find one to do it for free?'"

I laughed at her dead-on imitation of Diane.

"So, she didn't care?"

"Nope. And she said I didn't have to worry, that she was going to fire Linda the minute she came back into the office for acting so unprofessionally. And she shooed me out of her office, insisting I did nothing wrong."

"Did you get to see her getting fired?" I asked.

"Sadly, no. I was out at a showing. But my coworkers said it was great fun when Linda stormed out of Diane's office, still yelling. She packed some things in a bag and stormed off. Everyone stood and applauded."

"But you lost that house sale."

"No, Diane gave it back to me. I have three showings there tomorrow."

"Good," I said. "Listen, I'm sorry I got so upset at the awards dinner. I just felt so humiliated. I didn't know about Linda."

"That's why I wanted to explain myself to you. I'm so glad you talked to me."

I stood up and tugged her hand. She stood, too, and I wrapped my arms around her.

"Damn, I missed you, Brooke."

She squeezed me so tight, my ribs ached, and she started crying.

"I missed you, too. I've hardly slept!"

"I've barely slept. Liam says I've been a complete and utter idiot."

She let out a laugh that turned back into a sob, and started crying into my shirt.

"Oh, Evan. I love you so much. Please come back to me."

"I'm here, sweetheart. I'm right here. I love you, too. I promise I'll never let you go again."

And I kissed her, right there in the park, where everyone could see, and I didn't care. I lifted her up off her toes.

"I love Brooke Sinclair!" I yelled. "Take that, Linda!"

Brooke laughed, scaring a group of birds that fluttered away. The sky was so blue, and I saw it reflected in her eyes that looked at me with love.

EPILOGUE

It was August, and we were heading down to Boston for our weekend away. We left Vermont at two, and even the traffic outside the city couldn't dampen my mood.

Brooke had packed a giant suitcase for our two nights.

"I need to have options," she said.

I just packed some things in my small bag and hung some nice pants in the backseat of Brooke's car.

The day was warm, and we had the windows open for most of the ride. But when we hit the Boston traffic, Brooke asked if we could turn the air conditioner on, since the smell of exhaust was bothering her.

"Sure. Yeah, this truck in front of us smells awful."

I rolled up the windows and turned it on, and thankfully the truck pulled off at an exit a few minutes later.

The traffic got heavier, and it took a while for us to get off the exit, and then we practically crawled through town.

"Man, this traffic is awful," I said.

"I know. This hotel is wonderful, though. And it has a nice restaurant next door."

We finally got to the hotel, and a doorman came over to the

car to help us with the bags. I left to go park in the garage nearby, nearly gagging at the price for daily parking.

Brooke was waiting for me in the lobby with the key. We let the doorman bring up our bags. I tried to tell Brooke I could bring up the bags, but she liked getting the full experience at a nice hotel.

I gave the doorman a tip and closed the door behind him.

"Ohhh, this bed looks fantastic!" Brooke said.

And it did. It was king-sized and covered in a down comforter and loads of pillows. The room had a large, flat-screen tv and a small desk and chair. The bathroom was enormous, with a marble floor and two sinks.

"Would you mind if I took a nap?" Brooke asked. "I'm so tired today. It's been such a long week."

"No, I don't mind. Should I make dinner reservations?"

"Oh, it's too late to get reservations for tonight," she said. "I made reservations months ago."

"You think of everything."

Brooke kicked off her shoes and tugged off her pants. She unbuttoned her shirt and peeled it off. Then she walked to the bathroom in blue lace panties and a matching bra.

"Damn," I said. "Are you sure you want a nap before dinner?"

"Yes."

She closed the bathroom door. I took Brooke's laptop out of her shoulder bag, and I found my headphones. I hopped on the bed and brought up a movie to watch. Brooke came out of the bathroom yawning. I watched her boobs jiggle as she crossed the room.

"Is that a new bra?" I asked.

"Yes."

"I like it."

She rolled her eyes, then she unhooked it and took it off.

"Um, what are you doing?" I asked.

"I don't sleep in a bra. You know that."

She opened her suitcase and pulled out a t-shirt. I was sad to see her boobs disappear under the shirt.

"Night," she said, crawling under the covers on her half of the bed.

"Night."

I was almost finished my movie when she woke up. I took off my headphones.

"Did you have a good nap?"

She yawned and stretched. "Yes. Very good."

I finished watching my movie a few minutes later.

"Hey, do you think we should call Matty?" I asked.

"We just left a few hours ago. I'm sure he's fine. He's probably not even home from work yet."

"He's probably home now. Let's just call him real quick."

"Okay, if it makes you feel better."

I called him through the video chat on the laptop, and he answered.

"What do you want? I just got home like fifteen minutes ago."

"Uh oh, he's cranky," Brooke said.

Matty peered at the screen. "Is that Brooke?"

"Yes."

"Hey! Oh, gross, are you two in bed already?"

I laughed. "Brooke just took a nap, and I watched a movie."

"Oh, okay. Well, as you can see, the house is still in one piece. I'm having a big party tonight, though. At least two hundred people."

"Very funny. I just wanted to check in, since you left just as we were waking up this morning."

Matty went over to the fridge and looked inside.

"Sweet! You bought my drinks. Thanks, Brooke."

"Your welcome, baby brudder. I also shopped for extra snacks. They're in the pantry."

"Thanks."

"Don't forget to feed the cat," I said.

"As if she'd let me forget. Wait a second, she's right here."

Matty disappeared a few seconds, then came back holding Brooke's cat, Sammie. The cat blinked at us, then turned to snuggle into Matty's arms, purring. She was shy around me and Matty at first, but she grew close to Matty and usually slept in his room.

"Sammie likes you more than she likes me," Brooke joked.

"No she doesn't," he said. "She still loves her mommy. Okay, I gotta go. I'm going to the center later."

"Okay, I'll call you tomorrow," I said.

"Ugh, do you *have* to? Bye."

I turned off the laptop. "Well, the house is still standing."

"He's only been there for fifteen minutes. Give him time."

"Very funny."

I bought the grey ranch near the downtown park. I proudly paid the down payment with the money I had saved, plus the ten thousand that Brooke insisted I take. I was never so proud of myself as I was that day at the closing when Brooke handed me the keys and hugged me.

The house needed work, and Matty and I started working on it right away. We painted the living room and the bedrooms. We moved in Brooke's furniture, which was nicer than anything I had at Liam's apartment. We bought a new fridge and made plans to paint the kitchen cupboards. Brooke and I slept in the master bedroom.

I loved coming home to her every night. We cooked, watched TV, and held each other in bed. And every morning, I woke up and looked at her while she slept, wondering how I'd gotten so damned lucky.

Brooke sold her condo and made a nice profit on it.

We made a suite for Matty in the basement. We put up drywall and made a bedroom for him. And we enlarged the half bathroom down there to add a shower.

"Now he'll never leave," I said.

"That's fine with me," Brooke replied. "Baby brudder can live here forever if he wants."

Matty was doing great. He got a job at a landscaping company mowing lawns and doing yard work until he could find a good job in sports medicine. He gained some weight eating regular meals that Brooke and I cooked. His skin grew tan in the summer sun.

We made it clear that if we suspected he was using again, we'd give him a drug test and bring him back to rehab if it was positive. He went to counseling, weekly meetings for recovering addicts, and was volunteering at a teen center nearby. He had friends, and I cosigned a loan for a good used car for him to drive to work.

Every day, the hollowness left his eyes, and I saw my kid brother again, like he used to be before he started using. I was cautiously optimistic that Matty's worst days were behind him.

Brooke and Matty got along surprisingly well. Brooke showed him how to bake, and Matty fixed her computer. They had developed their own inside jokes and ganged up to tease me.

Last month, I bought airline tickets for mom to come out and visit us. I brought her home from the airport, and the second she saw Matty, she burst into happy tears, since she hadn't seen him in person for seven months.

"Oh, you look so good, honey," she sobbed.

We all know what she meant: You look healthy. You look sober.

You're alive.

Liam came around to visit and help us work on the house. We planned to update the electrical panel and put in some new windows. I cooked on the grill when Liam came over, and we ate on a picnic table in the back yard under a large maple tree.

Life was good.

"So, how many times are we gonna have sex this weekend?" I asked.

Brooke laughed. "How about we start right now?"

I whipped off my clothes and climbed back into bed. We rolled around the big mattress, kissing and stroking each other's skin. She pulled off her shirt. I kissed her and pulled down her panties. And then I licked her until she came, her thighs trembling.

I crawled back up and slipped inside her.

"Oh, baby," I said. "You feel so good."

We'd finally ditched the condoms, and I loved slipping inside of her bare. She felt so good and wet and hot. I made it last as long as I could, stopping to kiss her, to cradle her face in my hands, telling her how much I loved her.

And I came when she clenched around me, crying out until I was spent, and the last of her throbbing faded. She stroked my hair as my breathing returned to normal. I slipped off her and lay beside her.

"That felt so good," I said.

"Yes, it did."

She turned on her side to face me. Her cheeks were flushed, and her eyes were filled with love for me. Her hair was frizzy and messy, and in that moment, she looked so beautiful, I wanted to capture it.

"Hold on. I need to get something. Don't move." I grabbed two things out of my bag and brought them into bed. "First, I need to take a picture of you right now."

"Evan, don't! I'm naked!"

"Not a naked picture. Leave the blanket up like that. I just want to get a picture of your face."

I took the picture, then showed it to her.

"Oh, my hair is a mess!"

"I don't care about the hair. I love how you look right now."

"Just don't show that to anyone."

"I won't. And there's something else."

"What?"

I held up a diamond ring. It took her a few seconds to focus on it, and she gasped.

"Evan!"

"I'm sorry, baby, I was going to wait until we were all dressed up and ask you after dinner in the restaurant, or maybe down by the water, but I couldn't wait one more minute. I love you so much, Brooke. I want you to stay with me forever. Will you marry me?"

Tears sprang to her eyes, and she started sobbing.

"Is that a good cry or a bad cry?"

"Oh, Evan. Yes. Yes!"

Her hand shook when I slid the ring on her finger. She threw her arms around me.

"I love you," she said.

"I love you, too."

She held me until she stopped sobbing and wiped her eyes.

"Evan, there's something I need to tell you, too. And I was going to tell you this weekend, but now..."

"What is it?"

She took a deep breath, then exhaled. "I'm pregnant."

I laughed.

"You're joking."

"No. It's true. I missed my period last week, and my boobs have been hurting. And then, two days ago, I was on the way to a showing at nine in the morning, and I had to pull over and throw up on the side of the road."

"Gross. So, you're sure?"

"I bought a test and took it that afternoon in an empty house and got a positive right away. I stared at it and laughed and cried, then had to pull myself together for the showing. I was waiting to tell you this weekend."

"Oh, my God. I'm gonna be a dad!"

Warmth and happiness spread through my chest, and I couldn't stop smiling.

"You're going to be the *best* dad," she said.

"Matty's gonna love being an uncle. I can't wait to tell him. I can't wait to tell Liam and everybody! Let's just stay in the room all weekend, order room service, and never leave this bed."

She laughed. "Nice try. I'll have to get up and walk around. I have terrible heartburn."

I put my hand on her stomach, trying to picture Brooke with a huge tummy. She'd look so beautiful, I was sure of it. And now I had a picture of her, just before I proposed, just before I found out we were having a baby.

"That's why you needed a nap this afternoon."

"Yes. Some afternoons, I have trouble keeping my eyes open."

I hugged her again and pressed kisses on her pretty face. I loved this woman so much. I was crazy about her. I loved the way she held me, the way she kissed me, and the way her eyes looked at me with so much love.

I loved the way she took care of Matty, buying his favorite snacks and drinks. I loved the way she was helping make our little house into a happy home. I loved how I just knew she was going to be a great mom.

"I'm going to take such good care of you and the baby," I said. "Forever."

"Forever and ever," she said. "I love you, Evan."

*****

Thanks so much for reading! Please consider posting a review of Evan's Wish. Go to www.robin-stone.net/evanswish for links.

Turn the page for a preview of *The Landscaper*, Book 1 in my Landscaper Series.

THE LANDSCAPER

I was having impure thoughts about a client, and it wasn't the first time.

I loved Friday afternoons. It was payday, the day I saw my favorite client, Mrs. Tracy Dawson.

Tracy's husband left the house every morning dressed in a three-piece suit and didn't return until dark. Her days were filled with shopping, nail appointments, and lunches with friends. On hot summer afternoons, Tracy sat by the pool, reading magazines, chatting on the phone, and drinking fruity cocktails.

Tracy's friends came over some Fridays. They stayed in the house and did God-knows-what. Sometimes they paraded out to the pool and swam in their bikinis, showing off their tanned bodies and squealing with laughter.

I preferred days like today, when Tracy was alone.

The Dawsons lived at the end of a quiet road up on the hill. They had a sweeping view of the mountains. It was a modern home with five bedrooms, five baths, and seven thousand square feet of luxury. It had a home office, a home theater, and a gym.

A detached garage held three cars. A second garage held two more.

The backyard had a large pool and a one-bedroom guest house. The Dawsons employed a housekeeper, a cook, a part-time handyman, and my company: Bowden Landscaping.

I employed three guys—friends from college and the neighborhood. We took care of Mrs. Dawson's yard. And she took care of my fantasies.

Today she was reclining on a lounge chair in a black one-piece bathing suit. The suit was one of her more modest pieces, as long as she didn't bend at the waist.

Jacob, my best friend and first employee, raised his brows at me. I grinned, but looked down at the mulch I was spreading.

"The yard looks beautiful this year, Jacob."

"Thanks, Mrs. Dawson," he said. The tips of his ears turned pink when she spoke to him directly.

"Great job," I said. "You and the guys can take off."

Jacob pulled off his work gloves. "You sure? These mulch beds aren't finished."

"I'm on the last one. Go ahead. See you Monday."

"Thanks, Kyle." He picked up his rake and left. The guys called out their goodbyes, and a few minutes later the truck started up and pulled away from the house.

I wiped the sweat from my forehead. Five more minutes and I could head home for a cold shower and a beer.

"That was kind of you," Mrs. Dawson said.

I squatted and pushed the last of the mulch into place. "They work their ass— they work hard. Only twenty minutes 'til quittin' time."

Mrs. Dawson adjusted her chair to a sitting position. She pursed her lips and took a long sip of her red, slushy drink.

"You're a good leader," she said. "The men look up to you. I like that."

"Thanks."

I was single, but usually immune to the charms of my clients. Most of the wives worked or stayed in the house when the landscapers came to mow, hiding from the dirt and noise.

But not Tracy.

Tracy liked to watch.

And she liked to be watched, too.

My skin tingled when she was near. I daydreamed about pounding into her pussy, hiking her long legs around my waist. I'd fuck her while she dug her nails into my back and screamed my name.

I felt her eyes on me as I put my tools into the wheelbarrow. She wore large designer sunglasses, but I'd bet a day's pay her eyes were glued to my ass.

I looked, too, when her back was turned. I loved when she walked around the pool in bathing suits and high-heeled sandals. The sandals defined her calves and made her ass swing when she walked. Watching her emerge from the pool with her long, dark hair clinging to her skin made my insides clench.

Must be nice to swim and lounge by the pool all day. No room for a pool in my tiny yard. I rented a small apartment above a garage that held my landscaping equipment.

No money to spare for luxuries, either. I needed new tires for my work truck. I'd just ordered expensive parts for my lawnmowers, but I did the repairs myself. The economy hadn't recovered in this corner of Vermont. Customers called, apologizing, to cancel their service. Some of them started hiring their neighbors' kids to cut the lawn.

I hoped the Dawsons still had deep pockets. I needed their business.

Mrs. Dawson put down her drink and stood. She walked—no, slinked—around the edge of the pool and descended the steps into the water. She swam a few feet, then flipped over and wet her hair, her breasts bobbing. I tried not to stare.

"How about a dip, Kyle?"

"What?" I dropped my spade, and it narrowly missed my toes. Thank God for steel-toed boots.

"A dip in the pool."

"No, thank you, Mrs. Dawson."

She chuckled. "Please call me Tracy. How old are you, Kyle?"

"Twenty-five."

"I'm only thirty-four." She smirked. "How old did you think I was?"

Oh, no. I wasn't playing that game. It ranked right up there with does my butt look big in this dress?

"Don't know. Never thought about it." I'd thought more about swimming naked in the pool with her. I'd lift her breasts to my mouth and suck her nipples while the water cooled our bodies.

I piled my tools into the wheelbarrow, taking my time.

"Any hot weekend plans?" she asked.

Catching up with laundry. Going over business paperwork. Deciding which bills to pay and which to put off.

"Might go out for a few beers with my crew."

"What about your girlfriend?"

I pulled off my gloves and stuffed them in my back pocket. I didn't mind the flirting, but all talk and no action was getting old. She was bored, but I'd grown sick of the teasing.

"Don't have a girlfriend. Didn't have one when you asked me last week, either."

"I find that hard to believe."

She swam to the edge of the pool. Tracy was a natural beauty, with long legs and curves a guy could grab onto.

Straight, dark hair that looked silky to the touch. And a full mouth I liked to picture wrapped around my cock.

Besides being a knockout, she was kind to the help, and smart. I liked her.

Mr. Dawson was a lucky bastard.

I pushed the wheelbarrow toward my truck, feeling the heat of her gaze on my ass.

"Don't leave without your pay," she called.

As if.

I put the gear in my truck bed and closed the gate. When I walked back to the pool, she was swimming, her legs breaking the surface.

Where was she hiding the money, in her bathing suit?

"The water's perfect. I hate to get out."

I focused on the clouds while she swam over to the stairs and climbed out. But I watched as she emerged, water dripping down her body, her dark hair clinging to her skin. My cock stiffened.

I couldn't believe her husband left her alone so often. A guy's gotta work, but the housekeeper said Tracy slept alone two or three nights a week when he traveled for work.

If I was with Tracy, I'd strip off that bathing suit and fuck her so hard she'd have trouble walking the next day. I'd take her on dates and shower her with attention.

As much attention as I could on my limited budget.

I pictured Tracy clutching the headboard while I pounded her from behind. I'd grip her long hair in my fist and bend down to kiss her neck.

She picked up a towel and slowly dried her skin as she held my gaze. Was I going to stand here and gawk while she toweled off?

Yes. Yes I was.

I stuffed my hands in my front pockets, trying to camouflage the tent I was pitching.

"The roses are so pretty this year." She rubbed the towel over her thighs, then bent to dry her calves, giving me a clear view of her tits. "If you need more work, I can recommend you to my neighbors."

My cock pressed against my zipper. "Sure. Thanks."

Tracy dropped the towel and pulled on her cover-up. She tied it at the waist and headed for the guest house.

"Come get your pay."

She opened the glass door and entered. Friday afternoons, I'd usually wait at the back door of the house while Tracy produced an envelope. Most of my clients paid their bill by credit card, but the Dawsons paid cash.

I followed her into the guest house. Air conditioning cooled my skin. Tracy stood in the living room, looking through a pile of papers. The living room was connected to a small but modern kitchen. The walls and furniture were covered in pale fabrics. A short hall led to the bedroom and bathroom.

"Have a seat," Tracy said.

"Can't. I'm filthy. Appreciate the offer, though."

She pulled out an envelope. "Here it is. Your pay, plus a bonus."

Hot relief shot through my limbs. A bonus might cover a set of tires.

She stood at the desk, holding the envelope. I waited for her to bring it to me, but she gave me a devilish smile that made my spidey-senses tingle. I stepped closer and reached for the envelope.

Tracy held it just out of my reach, against her chest. Her tongue darted out to coat her bottom lip.

A bead of sweat slid down my temple. "Tracy?"

"My God, you're a specimen." Her gaze traveled over my chest, then down to the bulge in my jeans. "Are you in a hurry?"

I wiped my temple with the back of my hand. "No."

Another moment of hesitation. Was she breathing louder? She handed me the envelope, and I stuffed it into my back pocket.

"Thanks."

I waited, terrified and excited she was making a move.

"I'd like to get to know you better, Kyle."

She was standing so close, I felt her breath on my chin.

My pulse jumped.

Was she going to stand there and tease me? Or would she finally do something about the sexual tension that simmered between us all summer?

My questions were answered when she took off her cover-up, and dropped it on the floor.

Continue reading The Landscaper

ABOUT ROBIN

Robin started writing stories when she was five years old. She wrote essays, articles, and over a million words of non-fiction before turning to fiction in 2011. She watched erotic and contemporary romance authors having way too much fun, and after writing her first erotic romance, she was hooked.

Her imagination is filled with painters, landscapers, and carpenters. Robin's sex-positive books (M/F, M/M, and M/M/F) are emotional stories that keep readers coming back for more.

Robin lives near Boston and likes reading, travel, and eating good chocolate. She loves hearing from her readers. Visit www.robin-stone.net to see a list of her books and sign up for her newsletter.

ALSO BY ROBIN

Standalones

Delivery Man

Toy With Me

The Painters

The Carpenter

The Mechanic

Collections

The Blue Collar Collection

The Landscaper Series Box Set

The Landscaper Series

Book 1: The Landscaper

Book 2: Landscaper in Lust

Book 3: Landscaper in Love

Book 4: Landscaper in Paradise

Book 5: The Landscaper's Christmas

The Bullseye Club

Book 1: Evan's Wish

Book 2: Liam's Desire

No Limits

Book 1: Sharing Darcy

Hero Club - A book in Vi Keeland and Penelope Ward's World

Brazen Player

COPYRIGHT

Evan's Wish
by Robin Stone

ISBN: 978-1-944514-27-3

Email
robin@robin-stone.net

EDITING: Personal Touch Editing
http://www.aquilaediting.com/

FORMATTING by Robin Stone using Vellum

Made in the USA
Middletown, DE
07 October 2022

12243726R00104